CUSTOMER
SERVICE
EXCELLENCE
CSE
Kent
County
Council
kent.gov.uk

C161020401

SPECIAL MESSAGE TO READERS

THE ULVERSCROFT FOUNDATION
(registered UK charity number 264873)

was established in 1972 to provide funds for research, diagnosis and treatment of eye diseases. Examples of major projects funded by the Ulverscroft Foundation are:-

- The Children's Eye Unit at Moorfields Eye Hospital, London
- The Ulverscroft Children's Eye Unit at Great Ormond Street Hospital for Sick Children
- Funding research into eye diseases and treatment at the Department of Ophthalmology, University of Leicester
- The Ulverscroft Vision Research Group, Institute of Child Health
- Twin operating theatres at the Western Ophthalmic Hospital, London
- The Chair of Ophthalmology at the Royal Australian College of Ophthalmologists

You can help further the work of the Foundation by making a donation or leaving a legacy. Every contribution is gratefully received. If you would like to help support the Foundation or require further information, please contact:

THE ULVERSCROFT FOUNDATION
The Green, Bradgate Road, Anstey
Leicester LE7 7FU, England
Tel: (0116) 236 4325

website: www.foundation.ulverscroft.com

DEATHLY CHRISTMAS

Eve Masters and her partner, the handsome and steady David Baker, are planning their first Christmas together on the beautiful island of Crete. However, life in the village is turned upside-down when Jennifer Anderson, a newcomer to the village, is murdered. Yet again Eve's curiosity puts her life in danger, but she is still determined to solve the case. Will David be able to keep her safe, or will Eve's recklessness drive them apart?

Books by Irena Nieslony
in the Linford Romance Library:

DANGEROUS AFFAIR
DEAD IN THE WATER

IRENA NIESLONY

DEATHLY CHRISTMAS

Complete and Unabridged

LINFORD
Leicester

First published in Great Britain in 2013

First Linford Edition
published 2015

A catalogue record for this book is available from the British Library.

ISBN 978–1–4448–2514–5

Published by
F. A. Thorpe (Publishing)
Anstey, Leicestershire

Set by Words & Graphics Ltd.
Anstey, Leicestershire
Printed and bound in Great Britain by
T. J. International Ltd., Padstow, Cornwall

This book is printed on acid-free paper

1

Jennifer Anderson smiled with pleasure as she sat at home next to her exquisitely decorated Christmas tree enjoying a glass of full-bodied dark red Italian dessert wine. She thought how deliciously sweet it was and what a thoughtful gift it had been.

All of a sudden she remembered what she had brought back from that afternoon's Christmas party, so she jumped up and dashed into the kitchen. Rifling through her enormous handbag, Jennifer eventually pulled out a small package.

'There it is, thank goodness,' she sighed with relief.

She unwrapped it impatiently, and a couple of moments later there was a piece of fruitcake sitting on her kitchen work surface. It was generously covered in both marzipan and icing and Jennifer licked her lips in anticipation.

She had brought the cake back from Eve Masters's Christmas Eve afternoon get-together. Putting it on a small plate, she took it back into the sitting room and smiled again. Jennifer loved Christmas cake. In fact she loved all food, especially wonderfully rich cakes and pastries, large cooked breakfasts, fish and chips; in fact anything that was fattening. However, looking at the cake, Jennifer started to feel guilty. She knew she had eaten far too much at Eve's house, but how could she have stopped herself indulging in all those sumptuous dishes?

It had been an excellent spread, but despite Jennifer enjoying the food, she was certain Eve had been showing off her culinary skills. She hadn't known Eve for long, but she didn't like her at all and couldn't imagine what her partner, David, saw in her. Yes, Eve was a particularly attractive woman, but she couldn't believe that David was that superficial and had only wanted to go out with her because of her looks. In the end she decided that he must have felt sorry for her during the summer when the crazy Phyllis Baldwin had been trying to murder her. Yes, that was it, and now he couldn't get out of the relationship. He was too much of a gentleman to end things so soon after such a traumatic experience.

Jennifer looked at the cake again. She was sorely tempted to eat it, but her skirt was feeling tight and the buttons on her blouse looked as if they were going to pop open.

Damn that Eve, without an ounce of fat on her.

However, a few minutes later she was drooling over the cake again. It *was* Christmas after all, and a time for a little extravagance, so Jennifer thought that perhaps she should indulge now and go on a diet when the holiday season was over. However, what she'd forgotten was that Christmas was a little different in Orthodox Greece to what it was in England. The Greeks celebrated the time from Christmas Day until January 6th more than the days leading up to Christmas. Eve, and her arch enemy, Betty Jones, were trying to outdo each other with their organization of the celebrations for the next two weeks. The Christmas holiday season was far from over yet, and if Jennifer joined in the festivities, she would not be starting her diet for some time.

Managing to resist the cake for a little longer, she sat back, thinking how lucky she was spending Christmas in Crete. It was early evening in late December, but it was still warm and there was no need to have a fire or to put on the central heating. She had barely used any heating oil or firewood yet this winter and she was already planning what to do with the money she had saved. However, she wasn't aware that there could be weeks of rain and wind on Crete during January and February and that the concrete houses, which were very common on the island, both retained heat in the summer and cold in the winter. She could be digging deep into her wallet very soon.

Jennifer had moved to Crete two months previously after her elderly father had died, leaving her financially secure. She hated her mundane office job and decided to emigrate. Jennifer had been visiting Crete for many years and loved the peace and tranquillity of the island as well as the beaches, ancient Minoan palaces and the opportunities for long picturesque walks. She wasn't worried about the state of the economy in Greece. For her, the good outweighed the bad.

Eve Masters hadn't been living in Crete for much longer than Jennifer, having arrived in August, but she had managed to pack a great deal into her short time there. Just before she came to live on the island, a British estate agent, John Phillips, had been murdered in her village, and Eve, deciding that the Greek police weren't competent, managed to solve his murder, together with that of a holiday rep, Laura James. She also managed to survive three attempts on her own life when the murderer — the quiet but brutal Phyllis Baldwin — tried to silence her. To cap it all, Eve had fallen madly in love with the handsome but gentle David Baker, an author who had been living on the island for a few years. David had been fascinated with Eve from the moment he met her, but he had also been confused and bewildered by her. He had reluctantly agreed to help her find the killer and eventually realised he was in love with her.

Jennifer finally couldn't hold back any longer and took a bite of the Christmas cake. It was full of raisins, sultanas and cherries and had been soaked in brandy or whisky; she couldn't tell which. Whatever spirit it was, it didn't matter to her. The cake was absolutely delicious.

Jennifer took another sip of dessert wine and then lay back in her chair thinking of David. He was one of the most handsome and polite men she had ever met. He was at least six feet tall, with jet-black hair and piercing blue eyes. She had been excited to hear that he had been an actor before becoming a writer, and she was still racking her brains to remember if she had seen him on TV.

Starting to daydream, Jennifer remembered how much attention David had paid her that afternoon. She was certain he was losing interest in Eve. After all, Eve was a bossy and aggressive woman while she came over as a much kinder and more pleasant person. Granted, Eve was only forty-three while she was fifty-two and Eve did have perfectly cut blonde hair and rather attractive green eyes, but her shoulder length wavy dark hair and brown eyes weren't exactly off putting. Once she'd lost a bit of weight and had her hair styled properly, David would forget about Eve; she was sure of that.

Taking another bite of cake, Jennifer decided she wouldn't tell Eve how good it was. She didn't want to inflate her ego, deciding it was big enough already. Anyway, she was certain Eve hadn't baked the cake herself. She remembered Betty Jones had said that Eve wasn't the best of cooks.

Jennifer thought again about that afternoon and how lovely it was when David had asked her to dance. He had even kissed her on the cheek under the mistletoe. She smiled as she remembered glancing at Eve, certain that she was glaring at her. She was sure that the younger woman was seething with jealousy.

Jennifer then started to imagine what it would be like to steal David away from Eve. She could tell how pleased Betty had been earlier on when she had seen David dancing with her. Betty didn't like Eve at all and Jennifer had heard that she had tried her hardest to keep Eve and David apart in the summer. Unfortunately, it hadn't quite worked out, so Betty would be overjoyed if she managed to separate David and Eve.

Betty and her husband, Don, had lived on Crete for many years and were in their mid-sixties. Betty liked to take charge of the events involving the English community and had formed a drinking club in the Black Cat, an English bar run by Ken and Jan Stewart. Jennifer liked to be friends with important people in the community and had been delighted when Betty had invited her to spend Christmas Day with her and her husband.

Jennifer had almost finished the cake and there was only a small bit left. She decided to save that tiny piece for late evening. Eve certainly hadn't been generous with her precious cake and Jennifer could eat it all again. However, it was probably for the best. She didn't need to put on another ounce, not now that she had set her sights on David. She thought she'd finish her drink and then relax in front of the television, but as she reached over to get her glass of dessert wine, her head started to spin and she felt sick. Trying to get up,

Jennifer felt her muscles tighten and she couldn't imagine what was happening to her. She was terrified and tried to move towards the phone, but her body didn't want to do what she asked of it. She tried to speak, but nothing would come out. Jennifer felt fear overwhelm her, a fear she could never have imagined.

What's happening to me? Who did this? she thought. *I shouldn't have* . . .

However, her thoughts stopped as her neck and back began to arch and her mouth started to froth. As her arms and legs became rigid and her jaw tightened, Jennifer lost consciousness . . .

2

'You're not really jealous, are you, darling?' David asked Eve.

He put his arms around her as they stood next to her perfectly decorated Christmas tree. She had seen Jennifer's tree when she had gone to give her an invitation to her party and had decided that while Jennifer's was nice with its red and gold ornaments, her white decorations were decidedly more stylish.

Eve didn't want to talk to David about Jennifer and she grunted miserably, not saying anything. However, she didn't push him away.

'It was just a Christmas kiss,' he continued, looking slightly mournful. As much as he loved her, he still wondered why Eve had to make a big deal of everything. 'I think Jennifer's a lonely woman,' he continued. 'And she seems to hover around Betty all the time. We don't want her to turn into another Phyllis, do we?' David asked Eve, knowing this would strike a chord.

Eve shuddered as she remembered Phyllis Baldwin. Phyllis had seemed to be a fairly pleasant, quiet and nondescript woman who had unfortunately been at the beck and call of Betty Jones. However, she had murdered two people: first her lover, John Phillips, who had the audacity to end their affair; and then Laura James, who had known too much about that relationship. Then Phyllis had attempted to kill Eve because she had tried to discover who the murderer was. However, despite poisoning Eve, tampering with the brakes on her car and locking her in her basement while setting her house on fire, Eve survived all of Phyllis's efforts to get rid of her. Eve was lucky to be alive and was relieved that Phyllis was in prison and wasn't likely to be released in the near future.

'I know you were just being kind,

David,' Eve replied reluctantly, not liking it when David chastised her. 'But I'm pretty sure Jennifer's going to take it the wrong way. I've seen the way she looks at you. She's totally smitten. You don't realise how gorgeous you are, darling.'

David laughed and gave Eve a big hug. 'Nonsense. That's just how you see me. I'm nothing special. I'm an ordinary guy.'

David wasn't aware of quite how handsome and appealing he was to the opposite sex. He didn't possess an ounce of vanity and thought of himself as an average bloke, but not only did he have a particularly striking face, but he had a perfectly toned body as well, especially for a man in his early fifties. However, he didn't keep fit to look good, but mainly for health reasons. Each morning he would go for a long walk, often stopping at Eve's to pick up her dog, Portia. Eve also enjoyed walking, but she didn't much like early starts and she would walk Portia in the evenings. Two or three times a week, Eve and David would go into Chania, the nearest major town, and use the gym. Eve knew that now she was in her forties she had to make an effort to keep her body looking as good as it did. Unlike David, Eve was vain and went to great lengths to take care of her appearance.

'I'm sure she only thought of it as a bit of fun, Eve,' David continued. 'She knows we're a couple. Don't be so insecure. You know I only have eyes for you!'

David laughed again and pulled Eve closer so that he could kiss her. Eve couldn't help but kiss him back, but she did feel unsettled. She always gave the impression of being in control of her emotions, but underneath she wasn't as confident as she appeared. She felt David was playing with fire as far as Jennifer was concerned. From the moment Jennifer Anderson arrived in Crete, Eve felt she had set her sights on David, despite the fact that it was obvious that he was in a relationship with her. Yet again Betty had decided to interfere. Since losing Phyllis as a friend, she had been wandering around on her own looking miserable, but as soon as Jennifer had walked into the Black Cat, Betty had latched onto her. Eve believed she would like nothing better than to see David leave her for Jennifer.

'Come on,' David said. 'Everything's in the dishwasher so let's sit down and relax.'

Eve collapsed on the settee, followed by David. He put an arm around her and she cuddled up to him.

'I'm proud of you, Eve. You threw a wonderful party this afternoon.'

'I can't take all the credit; you did help a lot,' Eve replied.

'I know, but you cooked all the food. It was absolutely delicious. And to think you were barely able to boil an egg when you first arrived on the island.'

'That's going a bit far,' Eve said, looking slightly cross. 'But, you're right; I wasn't the best of cooks. I have been practising, as you know.'

Eve paused for a moment, trying to find the right way to tell David a secret she'd been keeping.

'David, I have something to confess,' Eve mumbled.

She sat up and David found he was slightly concerned. What had she done now? He had been through so much with Eve that he had got used to her wild actions, but he was hoping for a peaceful Christmas.

'Oh dear, I don't know if I can tell you,' she continued, looking a little red in the face.

'You can tell me anything, darling. I don't think I'd be too shocked by whatever you've said or done, not after last summer.'

Eve gave David a severe look, though deep down she knew she deserved this. She had suggested some crazy things when they had been looking for John and Laura's killer. One of her ideas had been to break into John's house and it had been sheer luck that they hadn't been caught. In addition, although Eve had become a more pleasant person since she had met David, she still had a tendency to be reckless.

'The cake,' Eve replied, looking down, filled with embarrassment. 'I cooked everything apart from the Christmas cake. I've improved so much with my cooking that I intended to bake a Christmas cake this year, but I forgot and then it was too late. I should have baked it in November, but before I knew it, it was almost Christmas. So I went to the English shop and bought a Christmas cake. That's awful, isn't it? Then Jennifer kept asking for a piece to take home this afternoon and I gave her such a small slice. She must think I'm terribly mean. Mind you, I don't know why I care. After all, she is trying to steal you away from me.'

David smiled and gave Eve a kiss on the cheek. 'Eve, you're so sweet. It doesn't matter about the cake. You did most of the cooking, after all. I'm sure most people cheat a little at such occasions. And as for Jennifer, I'm sure she'll enjoy the cake whether or not it's home-baked and whatever size it is. Don't worry about it. I'm still very impressed with your efforts today.'

David pulled Eve closer. He was looking forward to spending his first Christmas with Eve. They had thrown a successful party for all their friends that afternoon and now they were going to spend a romantic Christmas Eve together drinking mulled wine and opening presents. The following day they were going to have Christmas lunch at the home of their friends, Pete and Annie Davies. Slightly younger than Betty and Don, Pete and Annie had taken early retirement and had moved to Crete a few years previously. Pete had been a police officer and Annie a schoolteacher back in England and both had been very kind and helpful to Eve during the summer, especially after she had been poisoned.

'What are you thinking about, David?' Eve asked.

'Oh, just about us spending our first Christmas together.'

Eve smiled and moved closer to David. 'Yes, it is wonderful, isn't it? I think we should open a present now, don't you?'

Eve jumped up cheerfully. She was a woman who could never sit still for long. Not only did she like to be doing something, but her mind was always active and needed constant stimulation. David hadn't been sure he would be able to keep her occupied after the excitement of the summer murders, but he had been doing all right so far. However, unlike Eve, the turmoil and instability of the summer months had been too much for him and he was relieved that everything had quietened down.

3

Betty rang the doorbell for the third time. *Where on earth is that woman?* she thought crossly.

Betty wasn't known for her patience and she couldn't abide tardiness. Jennifer should have been at her house an hour ago, but she hadn't even phoned to say she'd be late. Betty had called her on both her landline and mobile, but there had been no answer and no reply to either of her messages. In the end she had decided to drive to Jennifer's house. She lived in the next village so it only took her a few minutes to get there, but Betty's temper was rising. She was in the middle of cooking Christmas Day lunch and was annoyed at this interruption, but her husband, Don, had twisted his ankle a couple of days previously, so wasn't able to drive and go instead of her.

Still standing at Jennifer's front door and getting no reply, Betty was now fuming.

Has Jennifer overslept? she thought angrily to herself. *After all, she was drinking an awful lot at the party yesterday. That will have to stop if she's going to be David's new girlfriend. It's uncouth and unladylike to drink like a fish. A couple of glasses of wine are fine, but certainly no more. That Eve can certainly knock them back. How David puts up with it, I don't know.*

Betty never stopped having a dig at Eve, whether her information was correct or not. In fact, while Eve enjoyed a drink or two, she never appeared drunk in public and always made sure she was in complete control of her faculties.

If Jennifer was indeed asleep, Betty thought that perhaps she should try and get inside and wake her up. After all, she would be embarrassed if she missed Christmas dinner at Betty's house.

Noticing that the shutters on the

windows in the front of the house were closed, Betty walked round to the back to see if any had been left open there. As luck would have it, they were all open and Betty breathed a sigh of relief. As is common in Greece, Jennifer hadn't put up any curtains. Betty didn't like that tradition and had put up curtains in all her rooms, but today she was relieved that Jennifer hadn't bothered. Now she would be able to see in, but she would have to have a word with Jennifer. It wasn't nice that anyone could look into your home and it was impossible to keep the shutters closed all day. The house would be dark and you would have to use artificial light all the time.

Peering through the French windows into the sitting room, Betty couldn't see anything at first. As her eyes became accustomed to the different light, she thought she saw something on the floor. It looked like a big sack and Betty wondered if Jennifer had dropped the rubbish.

No, it isn't . . . Betty gasped a moment later. *It's a person. Is it Jennifer? No, it can't be . . . . Yes it is. What's she doing lying on the floor? Has she fainted?*

Betty knocked gently on the glass, but Jennifer didn't move. She then tapped a little louder, but she didn't want to shatter the glass. When Jennifer still didn't stir, Betty became concerned. She tried to get her mobile out of her bag, but she was trembling and she dropped everything. Picking up her bag, she began to cry. Betty was surprised at herself. She very rarely wept, but after the recent murders she had become edgy and nervous. She stood there for a few minutes, not knowing what to do, and then looked inside again. Jennifer still wasn't moving, so even if she wasn't dead, she was most probably badly hurt.

Finally, managing to get her phone out, she realised she didn't know who to ring. Barely speaking a word of Greek, it would be too difficult to ring the police. Anyway, she wasn't sure if Jennifer was dead, so she could end up looking foolish if her friend had just fallen. If she rang Don, he wouldn't be able to get to Jennifer's house because of his twisted ankle, and anyway he didn't speak much Greek either. Perhaps she should see if the French windows were open, but she was terrified. What if Jennifer was dead? Betty was petrified of being so close to a corpse, but she had no choice. She stood there for a moment and then, taking a deep breath, tried the French windows. She didn't know how she felt when they opened, but nevertheless she went in, albeit nervously.

Betty slowly walked over to Jennifer, but when she reached her, she wasn't able to look down. She started sobbing again and a sick feeling overwhelmed her, but finally she knew she couldn't put it off any longer. Betty glanced down at the woman who was supposed to be her new best friend and David's next love.

Jennifer's face had a horrifically contorted expression on it and Betty realised straight away that she was well and truly dead. She knew she was going to be sick and she dashed into the bathroom as quickly as she could.

Coming out a few minutes later, she sat on a chair as far away from Jennifer as possible. She didn't know what to do, but then she thought of ringing David.

He'll take charge and sort this out, I know he will . . . Oh no, he's with Eve having Christmas lunch at Pete and Annie's. Still, that would ruin her Christmas. She smiled wickedly. *No*, she then thought, *I mustn't think like this now, not with Jennifer barely cold*.

Betty then thought of calling Pete, but as he and David were together she might as well ring David after all. They could decide between them who would come over. Both David and Pete spoke Greek quite well so either could ring the police.

Although Betty was still trembling, she managed to calm down enough to make the phone call. In the end she knew she couldn't take advantage of this terrible situation so she rang Pete, not wanting to make it look too obvious that she was trying to prise David away from Eve on Christmas Day.

Betty came straight to the point on the phone, not wanting to show that she was upset. She never liked to appear weak. 'I'm sorry to bother you, Pete. I'm at Jennifer's and she's dead.' She didn't think it worth giving a description of what the body looked like. He would see Jennifer soon enough. She hoped he would be there within minutes, as she didn't want to be there any longer than she had to be. It wasn't much fun being alone with a corpse, especially one as awful-looking as Jennifer's.

Pete also didn't mince his words, despite being shocked by the news, and told her to stay put and that he'd be there shortly. Meanwhile, Betty rang Don to tell him the bad news. He was worried about her being there on her own and told her to come home and get him. However, Betty didn't want her Christmas dinner to be ruined and insisted that he stayed at home and looked after it, giving him instructions of when to put on the vegetables.

'How can she think of food at a time like this?' Don spoke angrily to himself, waking their cat, William, who looked at him with an annoyed expression on his face. 'Poor Jennifer,' Don continued, the reality of the situation suddenly hitting him. 'She's only recently moved out here hoping to have a better life, and now look what's happened. What on earth is going on here, William? I thought we'd had enough murders for one year.'

William ignored his master. He was quite happy with his life on Crete and he settled back down to sleep, the smell of turkey wafting around the kitchen. He knew what treats were in store for him later and he had nothing to worry about. Don wished their lives could be as simple.

Meanwhile, Betty had another quick

look at Jennifer. What could have killed her? She looked absolutely revolting. It must have been a poison of some sort. Betty started to wonder who could have done it. After all, Jennifer hadn't been living on Crete for long and didn't know many people. Who could she have upset this badly?

Of course it couldn't be Pete or Annie, they're such a lovely pair and we've known them for years.

Then Betty thought about the new couple, Kevin and Lucy Fowler, a husband and wife in their late forties. They had moved over to Crete about the same time as Jennifer. Perhaps they had known each other before emigrating and there were hidden secrets in their pasts. Lucy was a small, plain woman who never said much, but Kevin was reasonably good-looking. He was quite tall, with dark wavy hair and blue eyes which had quite a sparkle in them. Betty thought he was almost as handsome as David, so he wasn't a bad addition to the ex-pat community. Betty thought it was always nice to have a good-looking man to cast your eyes over; and he did have the gift of the gab as well.

The Fowlers had come over to help Kevin's younger brother, Paul, with his gardening and maintenance business. Paul was single, in his mid-thirties, and in Betty's eyes not nearly as good-looking as his brother, but he had confidence in himself and was always flirting with the girls. Betty wondered how his business would do with the recession, but the ex-pats seemed to be taking him up on his services.

The doorbell went, rousing Betty from her thoughts. She jumped up and rushed to open it, relieved that she wouldn't have to be alone with Jennifer anymore. Opening the door, she saw both Pete and David standing there.

David is such a handsome man and so polite. If only I were fifteen years younger; Eve wouldn't have had a look-in. At that moment she had completely forgotten about her husband, Don. 'Thank goodness you're here,' she said, sounding more than grateful. 'I didn't know what to do. Honestly, my Greek isn't good enough to call the police.'

'Calm down, Betty,' David said, putting his arm around her. 'We'd better have a look at the body first.'

Betty felt herself tingling at David's touch. *Eve doesn't deserve such a kind, lovely man*.

They all went into the sitting room and the men looked at Jennifer. 'Looks like strychnine poisoning to me,' Pete said straight away. Having been a police officer, Pete was quite familiar with poisons.

'Oh my God,' Betty gasped. 'So somebody deliberately tried to kill her?'

'It seems that way,' Pete continued.

'Eve's cake!' she exclaimed.

'What?' David asked sharply, taking his arm away from her abruptly.

'There's a bit of her cake over there. The poison could have been in that. After all, she did think Jennifer was interested in you, didn't she?'

'Eve would never try and kill anybody,' David said angrily. 'I know you don't like her, but I love Eve and there's nothing you can do to change my mind about her.'

David's remarks silenced Betty. She knew she'd gone too far. He'd probably never forgive her. Why didn't she think before speaking?

'Now, now,' Pete said. 'We're all a bit upset. I think we should take a deep breath and try to calm down. It is a very traumatic situation after all. I can see that Jennifer had been drinking something as well. The glass is on the table and it hadn't been finished. The police will also need to test that for poison. And the sooner we call them the better, so that we can try and enjoy Christmas as best we can.'

'I apologise, David,' Betty said meekly. 'I don't know what I was thinking.'

David, who hated being on bad terms with anyone, accepted her apology. He knew Betty and Eve were never going to give up on their feud, and Eve herself had thought more than once that Betty was a suspect back in the summer murders. It was better to let it go. It was Christmas, after all.

4

'I don't believe it,' Eve exclaimed. 'How dare that woman accuse me of murdering Jennifer? Just wait until I see her. I'll have a few choice words to say. The only person I would ever want to poison is her . . . not that I ever would of course,' she added quickly.

'Calm down, darling,' David spoke soothingly to Eve, putting his arm around her. 'You know what she can be like. And admit it, Eve, you and Betty are never going to be friends.'

Eve grunted, knowing David was right.

'In all fairness, however,' he continued, 'she was in a state of shock after finding Jennifer's body. I can assure you it wasn't a pretty sight, and to top it all, Betty had been sitting alone with the corpse for some time before Pete and I got there. I think she spoke in the heat of the moment . . . and she did apologise in the end.'

Eve said nothing. She didn't like it when David made excuses for Betty. He, on the other hand, didn't know why Pete had mentioned Betty's accusations to Eve. He knew how she would react.

'Yes, please try to put it to the back of your mind,' Annie added. She was also a touch annoyed with her husband's slip of the tongue. You had to be particularly careful and watch what you said in front of Eve. There was no telling how she would react to anything, particularly if it wasn't supportive of her. 'Now come on, it is Christmas,' Annie continued, hoping that Eve would forget about Betty. 'Let's try and enjoy ourselves as much as we can under the circumstances.'

However, Eve was still livid. She had done her best to patch things up with Betty after Phyllis had been arrested. Phyllis had been Betty's only friend and Betty had naturally been upset to learn that she was the murderer. However, Betty had only been civil to Eve for a few days after Phyllis had been arrested, despite the ordeals Eve had been through. Betty had soon resumed her vendetta against Eve, refusing to accept that she and David were together. That had been the final straw for Eve and she had decided not to give Betty any more chances. The feud had been resumed with a vengeance.

However, as Annie had said, it was Christmas and Eve loved this time of year. She didn't want Betty to spoil it for her, and although the new murder had put a shadow over everything, none of them had known Jennifer well, so it wasn't as if they had lost a member of the family or a close friend. They were still entitled to enjoy the festivities, although they might now be a little subdued. However, unfortunately for everyone, a thought suddenly struck Eve.

'The police might suddenly turn up here,' she announced. 'That'll ruin

Christmas Day for us.'

'We have nothing to hide, so there's no need to be concerned,' Pete snapped.

Annie and David looked at each other. Pete rarely became angry and Annie realised that Eve must be trying his temper to the limit.

'What did they say when they arrived at Jennifer's?' Annie asked David, hoping Pete would become less tense.

Ignoring her husband was the only way she knew to calm him down. If she included him in the conversation, his temper would rise. Annie didn't want a bad situation to get worse, not on Christmas Day.

'Well,' David replied, 'the police didn't say much. They took our names and addresses and then removed the small bit of cake and the glass of wine that Jennifer was drinking. I believe they're going to test them both for poison. The body was taken away and that was it.'

'Oh my God, I've had an awful thought!' Eve exclaimed. She found herself shaking and her hands felt clammy. 'What if Betty's the killer and she went over to Jennifer's and put poison in my cake when she wasn't looking? Betty could have done it to put the blame on me.'

'Why would Betty want Jennifer dead?' David asked Eve, sighing with frustration. 'She was hoping to have her as a friend and confidante. Anyway, it looked like rigor mortis had set in so she couldn't have been killed when Betty went round this morning.'

'She could have popped over last night,' Eve continued, now having convinced herself that Betty was the killer.

'Oh come on, Eve,' David continued. 'Betty might be an unpleasant woman, but she isn't a murderer.'

'We don't know that. She's been acting very strangely since Phyllis was arrested.'

'Your mind's working overtime again, Eve,' David remarked, becoming impatient with her. 'In my opinion, she's a lonely, interfering and unhappy woman, that's all.' David knew she was being illogical, but the thing he was most worried about was Eve becoming interested in solving the crime. He had nearly lost her in the summer and didn't want a repeat of that experience.

Annie nodded in agreement. She had known Betty for a few years, but they had never become close. Annie found her too overpowering and manipulative, but she couldn't imagine her killing anyone, especially not Jennifer. Everyone knew Betty had chosen her to be her new best friend.

'I'm being punished for not making that cake,' Eve wailed a moment later.

Pete and Annie both stared at her, wondering what this was all about. Eve could be so dramatic.

'I made all the other food for the party, believe me, but I'd left it too late to make the cake, so I bought one at the English shop. Now I'm being punished.'

A few tears slid down Eve's cheeks and Annie went and put her arms around her, even though she knew her friend was trying to be the centre of attention again. 'Come on, Eve, nobody's judging you and you're not being punished for anything,' Annie said, hoping to comfort her friend and get her back into the Christmas spirit. 'It doesn't make any difference whether you made the cake or not. The fact you prepared everything else is outstanding. When you first arrived on Crete, you could barely cook at all. Now look at you. The rest of the food was delicious and it all looked as if a professional chef had made it. Wipe away the tears and let's eat lunch. We've got to try and enjoy the rest of today.'

Eve gently wiped away her tears, trying not to ruin her make-up, and attempted to smile. However, she was now incensed with the attitude of other people. Yesterday it was David, today Annie. Why did people keep mentioning that she couldn't cook when she came to live on Crete? She didn't think she'd been quite as bad as that. She'd put out quite a spread for her first party on the island and the only thing she'd bought pre-prepared was the pastry for the mini-quiches.

David thought champagne might cheer Eve up and lighten her mood, so he nipped into the kitchen while she was having a tirade about the awful food Betty plated at her parties. When he came back with the champagne, he evenly poured it into four flutes and Eve's face lit up. David was relieved.

'That's just what I needed,' Eve said a few moments later, smiling as she sipped her favourite nectar. 'I don't know why I'm getting so upset. It's what I've come to expect of Betty, so I shouldn't be surprised.'

Eve paused and then her face suddenly fell. David, seeing the change in her, found his feeling of reprieve disappear almost as quickly as it had arrived.

'Oh no, I've just had another awful thought!' Eve cried, the colour leaving her face despite her winter tan. 'Forget about Betty. Someone else at the party could have been trying to frame me. There were so many people there that it would have been easy for anyone to put poison in my cake and then get lost in the crowd.'

'Don't be silly, Eve,' Annie said quickly. 'The cake was in one piece for most of the afternoon. You cut the first slice for Jennifer, wrapped it straight away, and gave it to her. I watched you. The poisoner wouldn't have known which bit of the cake you were going to give her or if you were going to give her any. Then both Pete and I had a piece, so the poison can't have been in the cake. It was more likely in the wine, but we don't know where that came from.'

'But Jennifer put the cake in her handbag and left it on the floor for a while. I saw her do that.'

'Eve, it's better that we wait and see whether there was poison in the cake or not,' Pete stated, getting fed up with her obsessing about the cake. He had calmed down, but he could feel his temper rising again. Why couldn't Eve stop harping on? 'You're probably worrying for nothing,' he continued, 'and anyway, these were your friends at the party. I can't imagine any of them wanting to frame you.'

David went over and gave Eve a hug. In a way he was glad she was nervous. He didn't want her to become interested in searching for the murderer. She was lucky to be alive after the last time, but he knew that Eve's moods could change like the wind and she could recover from setbacks and her fears easily. He wouldn't be surprised if she forgot about her worries and went all out in her search for Jennifer's killer. She had very little faith in the Greek police, not to mention the fact that she would think of this as an exciting challenge.

'Come on, let's change the subject,' Annie said, wanting this conversation to end. 'Lunch is almost ready. I hope you two men can forget the image of the body.'

'It wasn't very pleasant,' Pete said. 'I did get used to things like this working in the force, but it must have been a bit of a shock for you, David.'

'It was pretty gruesome,' David remarked. 'I don't think I'll forget it in a hurry.'

It was Eve's turn this time to hug David. He was touched, especially as it was usually him comforting her.

'Right,' Eve said. 'Let's decide not to mention the murder throughout lunch.'

The others happily agreed, although they were surprised Eve suggested it, and Christmas lunch passed pleasantly enough, with an excess of food and wine. As they sat down in the sitting room afterwards, all thoughts of the murder had more or less disappeared.

'That was a delicious meal, Annie,' Eve said contentedly as she collapsed on the sofa. 'I'm well and truly full up; though I'm sure I can make room for one of those chocolates.'

Eve glanced at a large box of Belgian chocolates sitting on a side table, thinking that however full she was, there was always room for something sweet. Annie smiled, knowing that Eve would be back at the gym in the New Year making sure she hadn't put on any extra weight over the holidays; and if she had, getting it off as soon as possible.

Eve has a wonderful figure, Annie thought enviously.

Annie was also in good shape for a woman her age, but she didn't bother to exercise so she did need toning up. She kept meaning to go to the gym in Chania with Eve and David, but so far had made excuses. Perhaps it should be her New Year's resolution.

'Here are Metaxas for everyone,' Pete announced. 'I'm sure we've all got a little room left for these.'

Both Eve and David beamed, looking forward to their after-dinner drinks. They loved the Greek version of brandy, which was sweeter than the normal stuff. Annie went into the kitchen to make coffee.

Just as they had settled down with their drinks and chocolates, the door-bell went and they all jumped. 'Who on earth can that be?' Annie asked. 'Perhaps it's Betty and Don needing some company. I'd forgotten all about them and the murder. We should have rung them earlier to see if they were all right.'

Eve grimaced at the thought of spending time with Betty while Pete got up and answered the door. A few moments later, he came back in with two Greek police officers. Eve's heart missed a beat. *Not again*, she thought. She definitely didn't want to go through this again, having had enough of the police in the summer.

Eve recognised one of officers. When she was in hospital after being poisoned, he had been the one to interview her and he seemed to be in charge of this case. 'Good evening,' he said. 'My name is Dimitris Kastrinakis. I apologise for interrupting your Christmas festivities. I believe that Betty Jones called the two gentlemen here after she found Miss Anderson's body.'

'Yes,' Pete stated. 'Her Greek isn't

very good, so she needed help calling the police and I only live a few minutes drive away.'

'Miss Masters, we meet again,' Dimitris said, almost smiling. 'You are always around when there is a murder, is that not so?'

Eve, smarting at this comment, was going to tell him she had been nowhere near Jennifer's body, but Dimitris didn't allow anyone to get a word in and spoke almost immediately.

'We have spoken to Betty and she says you made the cake that Jennifer ate. Is that right, Miss Masters?'

Eve felt herself going red, knowing the truth would probably come out now; and once Betty discovered that it had been purchased from the English shop, she would revel in the knowledge. 'I'm afraid I didn't. I'd left it too late to make a cake. It has to mature, you see, and have alcohol poured over it every so often. It's the English way. So I bought one.' She noticed that Annie was trying not to smile and added, looking directly at her, 'I made everything else for my party. I only bought the cake. I opened it on the day of the party and sliced it in front of everyone, so I couldn't have put poison in it.'

'Well, the tests will tell the truth,' Dimitris continued.

Eve was about to argue with him when she felt David shove her in the ribs. He was probably right. It was better to keep quiet. Eve had learnt this the hard way in the summer.

'There is one other thing. Miss Anderson had been drinking dessert wine — we are testing that as well. Have you any idea where that came from? Was it a Christmas gift?' All of them shook their heads and said they had no idea if it was a present or not. 'Were any of you friendly with Miss Anderson?' Dimitris continued.

'I think I can speak for all of us,' Pete said. 'She was more of an acquaintance than a friend. She only moved to Crete in October. I think she was only friendly with Betty and Don Jones.'

'That's strange,' Dimitris continued. 'Betty said Jennifer was getting on well with you, Mr Baker.'

Before he could say anything, Eve piped in. 'Jennifer fancied David as a romantic partner even though he's with me. She was making a fool of herself, throwing herself at him. Betty encouraged her. She hates me, you know.'

David winced. Eve was making a good case for being the murderer. He knew she couldn't kill anyone, but as usual she wasn't thinking before speaking.

'Is that right, Mr Baker?'

'Well,' David replied, 'Jennifer did seem pretty keen on me. However, I didn't encourage her and I did make it obvious that Eve's my girlfriend. I don't understand why some people are hell-bent on stealing men or women who are committed to other people, I really don't.'

'Perhaps they think of it as a challenge, Mr Baker,' Dimitris stated.

'Now, Miss Masters, so far you seem to be the only person who has a motive to kill Miss Anderson.'

Eve felt sick and tried to think of something to say to get her out of the mess she had created, when Dimitris continued. 'However, I did get to know you during the summer and it would surprise me greatly if you had killed Jennifer. Nevertheless, you will remain on our suspect list. Of course it will be good news for you if your cake doesn't contain poison.'

Eve breathed a sigh of relief, but she was still a suspect and had an awful feeling that Betty would do anything to frame her for the murder.

'One more thing before I go, Miss Masters. No more searching for the killer this time. Remember what happened in the summer — you had three near escapes from death. You might not be so lucky this time.'

'Don't worry, sir,' David said quickly. 'I'll make sure she doesn't get herself into any sort of trouble.'

Eve gave David a nasty look which Dimitris caught. He imagined it would be highly unlikely that David would be able to stop Eve from doing what she wanted.

After the police officers had left, Pete topped up their drinks. Eve had become very quiet and David knew her mind was working tirelessly again. 'Eve,' he said quietly, 'you heard what the officer said. No interfering this time. You almost got killed in the summer. I love you and I don't want to lose you.'

Eve smiled, thinking how wonderful it was to be loved so much, but she was a suspect in this murder case and she was determined to prove her innocence.

5

On Boxing Day Ken and Jan Stewart held a lunch party in the Black Cat, their English bar, for all their regulars. The food was free and so were wine, beer and soft drinks, but spirits and mixers had to be paid for. They wanted to thank their patrons for their custom during the past year. Eve thought they were a little crazy giving complimentary wine and beer. While most people would be sensible, she was certain that one or two would take advantage.

Ken and Jan were in their mid-thirties and had moved to Crete four years previously. Ken was short and chubby with blond spiky hair, and Jan was tall and lanky and towered above him. Their light-hearted banter made them an ideal couple to run a bar, but everyone could see they were still very much in love with each other.

Betty and Don were the first people to arrive at the party. Unlike Eve, who didn't think it fashionable to be the first at any social gathering, Betty liked to turn up early so she didn't miss anything. She always wanted to know what was going on in the village and was known as a terrible gossip.

'Awful business about Jennifer,' Ken said, pouring Don a beer and Betty a glass of white wine. She had decided not to drink gin and tonics, her usual tipple, as the wine was free.

'Yes, it is. I'm still getting over the shock of finding her,' Betty replied. 'She looked horrific. Strychnine poisoning is not a pleasant way to go, I can tell you. She must have suffered dreadfully.'

'Yes, it would have been very frightening for her,' Ken agreed. 'Have the police any idea who did it? They did come over last night to ask us a few questions, but we didn't have much to tell them.'

'Well,' Betty said, 'it looked like she had been drinking dessert wine and eating Christmas cake. There was a little left of both, so the police took the remains. Eve made that cake, you know.'

'Are you insinuating that I poisoned Jennifer?' a loud voice spoke behind her.

Betty turned round to see a very cantankerous Eve glaring at her, with David quietly standing in the shadows. Eve had arrived at the Black Cat earlier than she normally would have done. She had been feeling restless all morning, still smarting at Betty's accusations against her. Eve wanted to have it out with her, despite David pleading with her not to.

'I didn't say that at all,' Betty replied indignantly. 'I only said you had made the cake. However, you weren't happy that Jennifer had been flirting with David, were you?'

'It was a bit annoying that she was throwing herself at him in front of my nose, especially at my house at my party, but it was hardly a reason for me to kill her. I'm quite secure in my relationship with David, thank you very much. Isn't that right, darling?' Eve said, turning around to smile at him.

'Of course, we're blissfully happy and Eve has no reason to doubt my love for her,' David replied, unusually vociferous in public about his feelings for Eve. Although David hadn't wanted Eve to say anything to Betty, he was getting fed up with her interfering in their lives and was inwardly pleased to see her shudder at his words. 'The police didn't seem to think Eve was the killer,' he continued, speaking with a much firmer voice than he would normally use. 'So please let this be an end to your allegations, Betty.'

Betty was exasperated. She didn't like it when David was cross with her. He was such a gentleman and she was desperate to stay friends with him, but he always stuck up for that irresponsible and reckless girlfriend of his. It seemed that if she wanted to be friends with David, she had to be nice to Eve as well, and she couldn't be; she just couldn't.

The door opened and Kevin and Lucy Fowler entered with Kevin's younger brother, Paul, in tow. Eve suddenly felt uncomfortable. Paul was a bit of a scoundrel and often put his arm around her and flirted, even though he knew she was David's partner. *What is wrong with some people?* Eve asked herself. *Why do they have to interfere in other peoples' relationships? Can't they concentrate on single people and not on ones that are taken?* David said it was harmless fun, but she didn't like Paul flirting with her, even though he was quite handsome with his light blond hair and sparkling, bright blue eyes. He was much too young for her anyway — what was he, mid-thirties or so?

Eve studied Lucy. She couldn't imagine being friends with her. Eve was trying hard to be a nicer and more sympathetic person, but Lucy was dull and Eve wasn't willing to give her a chance. It had nothing to do with Lucy being plain-looking; it was because she was utterly boring. She wasn't quiet, but she droned on and on about her children and grandchildren and nothing else. Lucy and Kevin had two grown-up sons and three grandchildren and according to her they could do no wrong. Eve always felt herself dropping off when she spoke, so she tried to avoid her whenever she could.

As Betty and Don moved away to sit down, David turned to Ken to order their drinks. Eve was satisfied with her confrontation with Betty, knowing that she had won. David had stood up for her superbly.

A few moments later Eve took a large gulp of her gin and tonic, having decided that now that her spat with Betty was over, the party was probably going to be a wash-out. Then the door opened again and Yiannis entered. Eve groaned inwardly. The party was not going to be boring; it was going to be a total disaster. Yiannis had been one of her prime suspects in the murders in the summer and he had never forgiven her for it. He still enjoyed tormenting her if he got the chance. Today, however, he ignored her and Eve hoped this would continue for the rest of the day.

Petros, John Phillips's old foreman, and his wife soon made an appearance as well, and then Annie and Pete came in with Jane Phillips, John's daughter. She was twenty-eight years old and Eve thought how striking she was with her jet-black hair and pure white skin. She had come to Crete to sort out her father's belongings and to put his house on the market. Eve thought how strange it was to come over alone during the Christmas period.

'Hello,' Annie said to Eve and David. 'I don't know if you've met Jane Phillips, John's daughter. I saw her in her garden earlier in the day and asked her if she'd like to come to the party. She's here all on her own. I knew Ken and Jan wouldn't mind.'

'I've seen you around,' Eve said, shaking her hand, 'but we haven't spoken. I'm Eve, by the way, and this is my partner, David.'

'Ah, you're Eve. Yes, I've heard about you. I think I have you to thank for discovering who killed my father.'

Eve blushed. 'Well, the police didn't seem to be making much progress, so I thought I'd give them a helping hand.'

'Well, thank you. I do appreciate it.'

'I'm surprised to see you here at Christmas on your own,' Eve said, her nosiness getting the better of her.

'I don't have any other family and after losing Dad, I didn't really feel like celebrating this year with friends, so I thought I'd just get away from England. Things needed sorting out here so it seemed like an ideal opportunity.'

'Good idea,' Eve said. 'No boyfriend then?'

David winced. Why did Eve have to be so inquisitive? 'Eve,' he said. 'Leave the poor girl alone.'

'It's all right.' Jane said, smiling. 'A few months ago I'd probably have burst into tears, but I'm fine now. There was somebody, but when I found out he was two-timing me, that was it. I thought he was special and believed he felt the same about me, but I was wrong. We all live and learn I suppose.' She looked a little wistful.

'I'm sorry,' Eve said, now feeling guilty for prying. 'I'm sure you'll meet someone much better soon. You're young and beautiful and should have no trouble whatsoever. I mean, I didn't meet David, the man of my dreams, until I was over forty! I was so lucky.' Eve put her arms around David and kissed him. He blushed, not liking so much attention being placed on him.

'I hope I'm as lucky as you, Eve,' Jane said enviously. However, she saw David's embarrassment and decided to change the subject. 'It looks like you might have another murder to solve now, Eve.'

'No, she hasn't,' David and Annie said in unison.

Eve looked at both of them grumpily, thinking that if she wanted to look for the murderer she would.

'Eve nearly got herself killed in the summer,' David elaborated. 'I don't intend to lose her so soon after we've found each other.'

'I can see your point of view,' Jane agreed.

'I'm old enough to make my own decisions, thank you very much,' Eve remarked severely. 'Especially as some people think I killed Jennifer. A little discreet sleuthing won't get me into trouble.'

'Oh Eve, I thought we'd finished with all that,' David sighed.

'Well, if you don't want to help me . . .'

'You're blackmailing me again, darling. You know I won't let you do this on your own. You'll get into too much trouble. Still, I'd rather you'd leave well alone.'

'We'll wait and see what the police come up with first and then I'll decide what to do. I won't do anything reckless, I promise,' Eve said gently, knowing that David was scared for her. 'Don't worry, darling, I won't jump into anything head-first this time.'

Eve took David's hand and Annie shook her head. She knew Eve meant every word she said now. However, she could get caught up in the excitement of the moment and become reckless, forgetting her good intentions.

Jane smiled. She could see that Eve was a determined woman and would listen to nobody. She liked her and wished she could be as brave as her, but she always thought out her actions before she did anything.

Soon everyone had their drinks and started to help themselves to the food. Jan put on some Christmas music and a couple of people even started dancing. Jane thought it a little strange to hear Christmas music after Christmas Day, but Christmas was different in Greece. Betty had been determined that the English community celebrated Christmas like the Greeks, and for once Eve had agreed with one of Betty's decisions. However, it was mainly because she loved Christmas and the longer it lasted the better. She had started the holiday season early like the English, decorating her house inside and out at the very beginning of December. Then she had taken a few days' holiday in London to see all her friends and the Christmas lights. And now, while England was already into the sales and advertising summer holidays, she could still enjoy the Christmas festivities.

A couple of hours later everybody seemed very relaxed and Jennifer seemed to have been forgotten. Eve and Betty had kept away from each other, Eve mainly because David had made sure that she didn't go anywhere near her. Eve and Yiannis also didn't cross paths, but Yiannis was hanging around Jane and both Eve and Annie were concerned.

'I don't like it, do you?' Eve said. 'We should do something.'

'I agree,' Annie replied.

Yiannis had bullied his previous girlfriend, Laura, so much that she had blackmailed Phyllis about her relationship with John in order to get money to get out of the country. In the end,

Phyllis had killed her.

'If we had helped Laura, she might have been alive today. I still feel bad about it,' Annie continued.

'Don't,' Eve said. 'I think it's highly unlikely that Laura would still be alive. Even if she hadn't blackmailed Phyllis, Phyllis might have thought her too much of a risk, knowing that she had seen her with John in Rethymnon.'

Annie was about to continue when the door opened and Dimitris Kastrinakis and another police officer came in. Everybody turned to look and the room suddenly became quiet. Ken turned the music off.

'We are sorry to disturb you,' Dimitris said. Both police officers looked around the room, studying everyone who was there. 'The only person in this room who was not at Miss Masters's party on Christmas Eve is Yiannis Neonakis. My assistant here will take you, Mr Neonakis, outside for questioning.'

Yiannis shot an evil look at Eve and she wondered what that was for. Had he really expected to be invited to her party? After all, they hated each other and he had threatened her more than once during the summer months.

Once they had gone outside, Dimitris continued, 'The strychnine has been discovered to be in the dessert wine. Each person in this room who was at Miss Masters's party has denied poisoning Miss Anderson or giving the wine to her as a Christmas gift. Someone could be lying, as it is highly likely that it is someone in this room. You, Miss Masters, are in the clear with your cake, but of course you are a suspect with everyone else for the wine. Nobody in this room is to leave the country until the murder is solved. We will be collecting your passports. And to you, Miss Masters, I will say this again: don't go looking for the murderer yourself.'

Everyone stared at Dimitris, dumbfounded. Their passports hadn't been taken away in the summer. Annie thought the Greek police must be getting fed up with the English and all these murders. Eve, however, was getting excited. She had hardly heard Dimitris telling her to leave well alone, but instead was looking around the room thinking of who had a motive to kill Jennifer. But did anyone? She knew so little about Jennifer, except that she had been interested in David. How was she going to find out more about her?

Eve's adrenalin was pumping. Life had been getting a little stale, not with David of course, but with living in a Greek village. It was okay in the summer when there were tourists about and everywhere was open, but in the winter too many tavernas and bars shut down and there was so little to do. Now she felt motivated again; but how was she going to persuade David to help her solve the murder?

6

The following morning Eve and David went to Chania airport to collect Robert, an old friend of Eve's, and Alison, Betty's niece, who were arriving from London. Robert had stayed with Eve during the summer and had helped her when she had been looking for John and Laura's murderer. He was an actor and had previously been one of Eve's clients when she had been a showbiz agent in London; that was, until they had a fling and she thought it prudent he found representation elsewhere. Robert was a strikingly handsome blond-haired man in his early forties who towered above most people. Alison was about ten years younger and was also quite stunning, with long dark hair and an hourglass figure. Betty had tried her hardest to get Alison together with David in the summer, but to her disappointment it hadn't worked out. As fate would have it, Alison had caught the same plane back to England as Robert and they had got on famously during the journey. They had started dating on their return to the UK and since then their relationship had become hot and heavy, much to Eve's relief. She could well imagine Betty trying to interfere again during this visit.

Robert and Alison had decided to stay with Eve, not pleasing Betty one bit. Alison had promised her aunt that she would spend lots of time with her, but she wanted to be with Robert and knew that they would have to sleep in separate rooms if they stayed at her aunt's. Betty was very old-fashioned and Eve had called her a prude more than once, though not to her face. David feared she would one day, causing more sparks to fly between the two women.

'There they are,' Eve called out, waving profusely.

'Hello, it's so lovely to see you again,'

Alison said a few moments later, hugging Eve first and then David.

Eve was surprised at such an open show of warmth. After all, they had been rivals for David's affections during the summer. Still, it had all worked out well for both of them in the end.

Robert then came along with the cases and gave Eve a big hug and shook David's hand. Eve thought he'd never looked happier.

'Well, I must say, you two look very relaxed with each other,' Eve commented.

'And so do you both,' Alison added.

'Yes, everything turned out fine for all of us in the end, didn't it?' Eve said, smiling.

'What you mean is, despite my aunt's interference!'

Eve laughed, but didn't say a word.

'Come on, let's get in the car and go home. I'm sure you're both tired,' David said, hoping to avoid a conversation about Betty.

Robert and Alison had taken the

overnight flight from Heathrow to Athens. They had then had a few hours' stopover in Athens before taking the fifty minute flight to Chania.

'Yes,' Robert agreed. 'I think we could both do with a couple of hours of shut-eye.'

* * *

Alison's eyes lit up when they got inside Eve's house and she saw her beautiful Christmas tree decorated with white ornaments. It was a living tree and as it still had roots, Eve planned to plant it in the garden after the festivities. However, her attempts at being ecologically friendly had ended at the planning stage. Eve fully intended that David would be the one who did the hard work of digging the hole for the tree!

Not content with one tree, Eve had bought a smaller one for the hallway, and there was a surprise for Alison and Robert when they got into their bedroom. There was another tree in there and both this one and the tree in the hall were also decorated with white baubles. Alison couldn't help but notice that the decorations looked expensive and the trees had been very elegantly dressed.

Apart from the trees, there were other decorations all over the house: Father Christmases, snowmen, wreaths; the list was endless. Eve hadn't considered the cost, but then money was no object to her. However, although the decorations weren't tacky and everything she had was tasteful and classy, Alison couldn't help but feel that Eve had gone over the top.

'Your decorations are wonderful, Eve,' Alison remarked nevertheless. 'They must have taken ages to put up.'

'They did, but I love doing it. Christmas is my favourite time of the year,' she said excitedly.

Alison thought Eve had never been so enthusiastic about a project apart from the murders, so perhaps it was worth the effort after all.

'Wait until you see the outside decorations,' Robert said. 'She used to go overboard in England, so I'm sure she's kept up the tradition here — or am I wrong, Eve?'

'I've put a few up outside,' Eve said, smiling, but not elaborating.

'That's Eve for you — always the modest one, aren't you, darling,' David said, giving her a hug.

They all laughed, knowing that describing Eve as unpretentious or humble was as far from the truth as you could get.

'Does anyone want a cup of tea?' Eve asked, ignoring them.

They did, and once they had sat down with their tea and biscuits, Eve started to talk enthusiastically. She had been waiting impatiently to tell them what had happened over Christmas, but had decided to hold back until they were sitting down at home and had her undivided attention. David knew how desperate she had been to tell them about the murder and had marvelled at her ability to keep the news to herself for so long.

'Well,' Eve said, 'I have some very exciting news.'

David sighed, wondering if 'exciting' was the right word to use about Jennifer's death. Robert and Alison looked at her expectantly, but both had a feeling of foreboding. Robert was beginning to think that he might not be going to have a quiet holiday celebrating a Greek Christmas and New Year after all. Something out of the ordinary had obviously happened.

'There's been another murder,' Eve blurted out.

Robert and Alison gasped. He was stunned and couldn't think of what to say for a moment, remembering the day he was in Eve's car when the brakes had been tampered with and he thought they were going to die.

'Aunty didn't tell me about this. Who was killed?' Alison asked, realising that Robert was lost for words. She was surprised to see how shocked he was, but then remembered Robert was involved in that car 'accident' with Eve. He probably didn't want to get caught up in another murder.

'It only happened on Christmas Eve,' Eve continued. 'In fact it was your aunt who discovered the body on Christmas Day, Alison. The woman who was murdered, Jennifer Anderson, was supposed to have lunch with your aunt and uncle, but when she didn't turn up and didn't answer the phone, Betty went over to her house and found her body. It was strychnine poisoning, apparently. And do you know what? Betty had the audacity to insinuate that I poisoned Jennifer. Can you believe it? She ate a piece of my Christmas cake before she died, you see. However the poison was in the dessert wine she was drinking, but nobody knows if it was a gift or who gave it to her if it was.'

'You're not thinking of looking for the killer, are you, Eve?' Robert asked glumly. 'Remember what happened last time. You could so easily have died.'

'Of course she is,' David piped in before Eve could say anything. 'Even though the police have warned her not to.'

'You should take their advice,' Alison said. 'You escaped death so many times in the summer. You could be tempting fate.'

'Well, I have you three to help me now. It'll be so much easier with all of us.'

'We'll all be in danger more like,' Robert said despondently.

'That's what I've been saying,' David agreed. 'But will Eve listen . . . '

Eve pulled a face. She wasn't going to give up, whatever anybody said.

'Well,' Alison remarked, 'I'd love to hear more about it, but I haven't had a wink of sleep all night and nor has Robert, so do you mind if we have a few hours in bed? We can talk about it later. We need to be awake for Aunt Betty's do tonight. You know what she's like!'

Eve grimaced. She wasn't much

looking forward to Betty Jones's Christmas do that evening. She knew Betty was going to go all out to outdo her Christmas Eve party. And to top it all, it didn't look like Robert and Alison were particularly interested in helping her solve the murder. She was certain David would be relieved about that and would expect her to forget about it. Well, she wasn't going to, even though it seemed as if she was on her own in trying to find Jennifer's killer.

* * *

Robert, Alison and David waited impatiently in the sitting room for Eve that evening. As usual, she was taking ages doing her make-up and choosing what to wear.

'Come on, Eve,' David shouted up the stairs. 'I know you like to be fashionably late, but this is going a bit far.'

'I won't be a minute,' Eve called back, slightly annoyed at being rushed.

She wanted to get her make-up and hair just right for Betty's party. She knew she shouldn't do it, but she wanted to outshine Betty. *Well, Betty's so horrid to me. She deserves it*, Eve thought, trying to justify her actions. In fact she had no need to go to such lengths to make Betty jealous. Eve was a highly attractive woman even without make-up on, and after all, she was twenty years younger than Betty.

Eve had put on her little black dress for this evening. It was short and fitted the curves of her figure perfectly. Despite indulging in food and wine over Christmas, she didn't show any signs of it and looked as slim as ever. There hadn't been much winter yet and Eve had managed to keep some of her tan, so she didn't need to wear tights or stockings. Her legs were still a delicate shade of brown.

Finally, Eve walked down the stairs and David gasped. He still couldn't believe how beautiful she was and that she wanted him and nobody else. Yes, she could be a frustrating woman at times, but she had an exquisite face and a stunning figure, and my goodness, he didn't think he'd ever loved a woman like this before.

David took Eve's arm and whispered in her ear how beautiful she was. Alison and Robert looked at each other and smiled. Both remembered the previous summer when both Eve and David were playing games, pretending not to be interested in each other. Alison and Robert were glad that they had finally come to their senses.

* * *

There were quite a few people at Betty and Don's house when Eve and the others arrived. Betty barely acknowledged Eve, rushing to hug Alison. Eve smiled to herself, thinking that Betty was probably jealous of the way she looked.

Eve studied the food, noting how much Betty had prepared. She thought

Betty had gone overboard trying to outdo her Christmas Eve spread, but didn't think she had succeeded. There was possibly more food, but it wasn't as sophisticated or upmarket as hers had been. Eve then studied the Christmas decorations. Betty had attempted to outdo her again, and although she might have had as many indoors as Eve, she certainly didn't have nearly as many lights outside. In addition, the Christmas tree was artificial and the baubles were a mixture of colours, which Eve thought was terribly unsophisticated and tacky.

Eve saw Jane standing alone in a corner and went over to talk to her. 'Hello again. Nice to see you out and about.'

'I wasn't sure whether to come or not,' Jane replied. 'I don't much like going to parties where I don't know many people, but I must admit I was getting a little lonely in that house on my own. I thought it would do me good to spend time alone. I didn't want to celebrate Christmas this year without Dad around, but I think I made a mistake.'

'Yes, sometimes we think we know what we want, but in the end it's the exact opposite!'

'And now we can't leave the country as the police have taken our passports. I wonder how long they'll keep them.'

'I have no idea,' Eve replied. 'Probably until we're individually ruled out as a suspect, but that could be a long time. I don't think the police have any idea who killed Jennifer, not that I've heard anything new. Have you?' Eve asked.

'No, I haven't, unfortunately.'

David came over with their drinks. 'Not talking about the murder again, are you?' he asked, looking anxious.

'Yes, but only because Jane's wondering when we'll get our passports back. She's stuck here until then. By the way, where's Alison and Robert, darling?'

'Alison's still having a reunion with her aunt. I think Betty's having a go at her for not staying here. Robert was chatting to Don a few minutes ago.'

'Can't Betty just be happy to see her niece? Oh, that woman!' Eve said crossly, trying to keep her composure.

David gave Eve a hug, hoping to calm her down. He didn't want a confrontation between Betty and Eve this evening.

A couple of minutes later, Don went to answer the door and a stranger stood there waiting to come in. The front door led straight into the sitting room and everyone turned and stared. The man was rather good-looking and they all wondered who he was.

'James,' Don said. 'Come in.'

'Thank you,' he replied in a deep husky voice.

Wow, what a wonderful voice, thought Eve. *An actor, perhaps?*

'Who on earth is that?' Annie whispered to Pete. He had no idea and shrugged his shoulders, slightly jealous of his wife's admiring glances.

'What a striking man. Do you know

who he is?' Jane whispered to Eve.

'He is rather handsome, but I've never seen him before,' Eve replied. 'And his voice — my goodness, how sexy is that?'

David was standing behind Eve and he frowned. They were in a committed relationship and here she was swooning over another man. He hoped Betty hadn't seen Eve drooling all over him. He didn't want that awful woman to come over and tell him she had been right about Eve. David knew Eve was probably only looking, but he still wished she hadn't thought him handsome.

Don was now going around the room introducing James, so David moved closer to Eve. She smiled at him and he breathed a sigh of relief. She *had* only been admiring the man, not planning to make a move on him. David knew he should be more secure in his relationship with Eve, but it was difficult. She was beautiful and he was certain many men were attracted to her. She was bound to find other men good-looking — it was only natural — but he was sure she remained faithful to him.

'I wonder who this mystery man is, David?' Eve asked. 'Don and Betty didn't mention they were inviting anyone new. I've not seen him before.'

'Me either,' he answered abruptly. 'Anyway, why should Betty tell you who she's inviting? She can't stand you.'

Eve was surprised to hear David speak to her in such a manner. What was up with him now? She couldn't be bothered with him at the moment though. She was more interested in finding out who the stranger was.

Finally, Don came round to Eve, Jane and David. 'I'd like to introduce you to Eve Masters and David Baker who live here, and Jane Phillips, who is visiting. This is James, Jennifer's nephew.'

'Oh, I'm so sorry for your loss. It must have come as a terrible shock,' Eve piped up straight away before anyone could get a word in edgeways. 'You were lucky to get over to Crete so quickly, seeing as it's the holiday period.'

David felt embarrassed. Eve, as usual, was taking over the conversation. *But what if she really does like him? Is this the end for us? Has she forgotten about our relationship already?*

'Thank you for your kind words,' James replied, his deep blue eyes sparkling. 'Yes, I caught the first plane out of London this morning. I want to make sure everything is done properly and the killer brought to justice as soon as possible. I don't completely trust these foreigners.'

David sighed. Eve and James already had something in common. She had little faith in the Greeks either. David was becoming despondent.

'I have a feeling I've heard of you, Miss Masters,' James continued.

'It was probably in connection with the murders in the summer,' David commented, before Eve could brag about her success as an amateur sleuth. 'Eve discovered who the killer was and almost lost her own life while doing it.'

'One of the people murdered was my father,' Jane quietly put in.

She found she was attracted to James and didn't want to be left out of the conversation, but feared her unobtrusive personality pushed her into the sidelines where she would be hardly noticed.

James glanced at Jane. She was beautiful, very beautiful, but she was quiet and probably a little young for him. Yes, he could easily be attracted to her, but if he was going to get involved with anyone, she needed to be confident and outgoing, and happy to accompany him to business dinners and so on. James didn't think this was Jane's cup of tea. Somebody like Eve was a more suitable candidate, but she was taken and her partner looked like he was going to explode if he carried on talking to her. Still, it was Eve who was flirting with him, not the other way round — if she really was flirting. James imagined that Eve liked to be centre stage and wanted to know everything about everybody. She was probably only gathering information about him. James decided to talk to Jane for a moment and let the situation between Eve and David defuse.

'I'm sorry,' James said to Jane. 'It must have been a difficult few months for you. Do you plan to move here?'

'No, I'm staying in England. I came over to get my dad's things and to put his house on the market.'

Jane was trembling. James was like no other man she had met, but he seemed more interested in Eve. It wasn't fair. Women like her always had men following them. Why couldn't she have the same confidence, not to mention Eve's style and glamour? Jane was shy and retiring and she felt that took so much away from her looks. Men were drawn to Eve because she conquered any room she walked into. Why couldn't she do the same?

Betty had been watching the group and wasn't happy that James was over with Eve and that she was dominating his attention. *That woman! Isn't one man enough for her? Well, she's certainly not having James, even if it would free up David. James is too good for her as well. I shall have to break this up*, she fumed. She stormed over to James and put on a very large smile. 'I hope these people aren't taking up too much of your time. You haven't met Annie and Pete yet. They're a lovely couple. You must come and I'll introduce you.'

'Well, folks, it's been a great pleasure meeting you all. I'm sure I'll speak to you again soon.'

'Yes,' Eve replied. 'It's been lovely talking to you, James.' Eve turned to Jane when he had left. 'So, I can see you like James.'

'What?' she mumbled. 'Was it that obvious?'

'Oh, I doubt if James noticed, but I could tell. I saw you tremble a little; am I right or not?'

Jane blushed. 'I doubt if he even noticed me with you here.'

'Me? I'm not on the market, so there's no point him pursuing me. I've got my darling David.'

With that, Eve went and put her arms around David and kissed him gently, not wanting to ruin her lipstick. Betty was watching and grimaced, realising it would be very difficult to split those two up. However, she refused to believe it was impossible.

James also watched the kiss and saw that Eve was well and truly taken, but luckily for him, he did also like Jane. She was a highly attractive girl, though lacking in forcefulness. James liked dynamic women, but perhaps he should give Jane a chance. It might take a little time and tutoring, but she could become the woman he wanted.

James suddenly remembered why he was here on Crete. What on earth was he doing thinking of women at a time like this? His aunt was dead; and worse still, she had been murdered, and it could have been by someone in this room.

Annie and Pete soon joined Eve and David and Jane's mind then started to wonder. She wasn't that good at small talk and she kept stealing glances at James. He was striking with his jet-black hair, just like hers, but his skin was darker and he was a good foot taller than she was. His eyes were a shimmering blue, while hers were a deep brown. She wondered what it would be like to gaze into his eyes, but what was the point thinking about him? She knew she was being silly. James didn't like her in that way and probably never would. Her last relationship had been a disaster and she was nervous about going into another one. Still, she missed being close to someone, but a man like James was way out of her league.

Jane then wondered about his relationship with his aunt.

Jennifer wasn't a nice woman, she remembered.

Jane had walked by Jennifer's house a couple of days after she had arrived and had spoken to her. It was nothing important, just pleasantries, but Jennifer had been short with her and had been uninterested in starting a conversation. Jane had heard she had been rude at Eve's party as well, flirting with David when she knew Eve and David were a couple. It was particularly impolite, as she was in Eve's home. How did she think she'd have a chance against Eve anyway? Eve was stunning, with a perfect figure, while Jennifer had been plain and was no spring chicken.

Jane sighed, wishing again that she could attract everyone's attention when she entered a room, just like Eve could. She couldn't think of any way that she would be able to entice James.

'What's up?' a voice whispered in her ear.

'Oh, nothing, Eve. I was just daydreaming,' Jane replied, blushing.

'I knew it — you are quite taken with James aren't you, Jane?'

'He is very good-looking, but he barely noticed me. I don't think I'm the type of woman a man like that would even look at.'

'Nonsense. Don't put yourself down. Yes, you are quiet, but that doesn't mean you're uninteresting.'

David, who was listening, smiled. There was a time when Eve thought that shy, retiring people were boring. She certainly had moved on and grown up.

'Perhaps a bit of a makeover might give you the confidence you need. What do you say?'

'It would be nice, but I may never be in this sort of social situation again, you know, where I might see James.'

'Tomorrow we're going to the posh Italian restaurant in Chania for dinner. It's all part of the Christmas festivities. I'll find out if James is coming. It would be an ideal opportunity for you two to get to know each other. You could really dress up for that. I'll help you.'

'I don't know . . . '

'Nonsense. It's a great idea.'

Suddenly a loud voice silenced

everybody. 'My aunt's killer will be brought to justice; that I guarantee.'

Everybody turned to look at James. He looked like a man with a mission.

7

Eve and David decided to leave the party earlier than Alison and Robert. James had gone back to his hotel shortly after his announcement, much to David's relief; but after having sampled some food and a couple of drinks, both David and Eve found themselves getting bored. Eve decided they were spending too much time with the same people over the holidays, but it had all been planned beforehand and she had got caught up in trying to outdo Betty with the arrangements. Now she was regretting making so many commitments.

Eve was also not having any luck that evening gathering clues about the murder and she was finding it frustrating. Nobody seemed to have a motive for killing Jennifer and she wanted to call it a day. Perhaps she'd have better luck after a good night's sleep.

David and Eve walked home, leaving the car for their guests. Eve thought it was marvellous that car insurance in Greece covered anybody whom the owner allowed to drive the car, thinking it gave you much more freedom, particularly if you had a glass of wine too many.

It was only a fifteen-minute hike back home, but Eve had forgotten she had the wrong shoes on for an uphill walk until they were halfway home.

'Well,' she said, finally collapsing on her settee and rubbing her feet, 'this murder is going to prove harder to solve than the last ones, don't you think, darling?'

'Yes,' David replied quickly. 'So it would be much better left to the police, don't you think?'

Eve ignored him, carrying on with her train of thought. 'The list of suspects is pretty small, isn't it? The police say the poison was in the dessert wine, but the question is, who gave it to her? She was only friendly with Betty and Don and I don't think either of them did it, do you?' she continued, not giving David time to reply. 'As much as I despise that woman, in all honesty I can't believe Betty is a murderer. Don is a gentle and quiet man and I don't think he has a motive. And Annie and Pete are our friends and I know it can't have been either of them. You had a go at me last time for suspecting Ken from behind the bar and it is unlikely to be him or Jan. Of course it could be any of these people if Jennifer knew something unpleasant about their past. And then it could be Betty if she found out that Don had been having an affair with Jennifer. What do you think?'

'I think it's very unlikely that Don would have an affair with anyone, Eve, and the same goes for Pete and Ken, before you mention either of them.' He sighed, thinking that Eve might cause rifts again between them and their friends. She had done so during the summer and he didn't want her to repeat that mistake.

'Of course we have Yiannis,' Eve went on. 'Now he has a foul temper. He could have made a pass at Jennifer and when she rejected him, took his revenge. Do you think that's possible, David?'

'It's extremely doubtful. Yiannis is only thirty and he likes his women younger than him.'

'That's true, but you never know with him. He's a very strange man.'

'Please don't go getting involved with Yiannis again. You know how awful he can be.' David shuddered, remembering Yiannis lunging for Eve a few months previously when she had upset him.

'All right, I won't; I doubt if he has anything to do with this, anyway. I suppose the murderer could be Kevin or Lucy Fowler . . . or his brother, Paul. It wouldn't surprise me if it was Paul, you know. He was looking after Jennifer's garden before she moved in and she dismissed him straight away. He could have been angry with her. I'm sure he needs every bit of business he can get.'

'That's hardly a motive for murder, darling.'

'People have murdered for less, David. Oh, I don't know. I must be losing my touch,' Eve spoke miserably. 'I feel like I'm a bit out of my depth this time.'

'I wish you'd forget about the murders, Eve' David said, shaking his head. 'I'd hate to lose you. I've got used to having you around!'

Eve scowled at David and told him to get her a drink.

* * *

Half an hour later, the doorbell rang and David got up. 'Who on earth can that be?' he said, with a tinge of annoyance in his voice. 'We gave Alison and Robert their own key so it can't be them, and we saw most of our friends at the party, so why would anyone want to talk to us again?'

'Oh, get rid of whoever it is,' Eve said, sipping a metaxa. She didn't particularly want to see anyone. Eve had had enough of socialising for one night, but a moment later she heard David talking to another man and was sure it was James. She suddenly felt revitalised and jumped up. She was about to rush to the door to make sure David didn't tell him to go, when both men came into the sitting room.

'Eve, James would like a quick word with you.'

She noticed David seemed even more annoyed, if not slightly angry, and wondered if he was jealous. There was no need for him to be this way, even though it was quite flattering. Eve didn't want anyone but David, although she found James very handsome and a touch mysterious. There was no harm looking at other men, as long as that was all you did. However, perhaps David was simply irritated because James had the audacity to turn up at this time of night.

'Good evening, Eve. I'm sorry to

bother you at such a late hour, but I would like some help from you if possible,' James asked with that husky voice of his.

Definitely should have been an actor, thought Eve. 'From me?' she exclaimed. 'I can't imagine how I can help you, but of course if there is any way I can assist, I would be delighted.'

David cringed. Eve was fawning all over him. They would have to have this out after James left; and the sooner he went the better. *The man is too young for her as well*, thought David. *What is he, mid-thirties? How can Eve do this, and right in front of me as well?*

'Well,' James spoke slowly and clearly, 'I'm afraid I don't have great faith in the police finding my aunt's killer. You did so much better than they did in the summer, and I was wondering if you would help this time.'

'I would love to,' Eve said quickly.

'I don't think it's a good idea,' David interjected. 'Eve nearly lost her life a few months ago. It's too dangerous.'

'Poppycock!' Eve exclaimed. 'Take no notice of David. I'll be fine. However, I did take a few too many risks in the summer; I will admit that. I will be more careful this time,' she said pointedly, looking at David.

'If you're sure . . . ' David knew there was nothing he could do except keep an eye on her. She had a mind of her own and would do whatever she wanted.

'Well,' Eve continued, 'have the police given you any idea of who they think might have killed your aunt?

'None whatsoever. I don't think they have a clue. What about you?'

'There seem to be very few suspects at the moment,' Eve said, shaking her head regretfully. 'But it's early days yet. Tomorrow night we're all off to the posh Italian restaurant in Chania, so I shall be talking to people again. Hopefully I'll be able to gather some more information. Are you coming, James?'

'I don't know,' he replied. 'Betty asked me, but I don't think so. It feels like I'll be celebrating the Christmas season a little too much after my aunt's death.'

'I think it could be advantageous, James. Kevin, Lucy and Paul Fowler will all be there, so we can get their reactions to you. They weren't at Betty's party, so this will be the first time you'll all meet.'

'Very well, I'll come,' James replied. 'Would it be all right if I get a ride there with you? Betty offered me a lift if I went, but I'm finding her too overbearing. I do have a hire car, but I don't know Chania at all and would probably get lost.'

'That'll be fine. We'll pick you up at seven thirty,' Eve said straight away. 'Oh, where are you staying?'

'The Sea View Rooms. Only place in the area I could find open at this time of year. But I'll walk here. I like a bit of exercise.'

'Fine, get here at about seven thirty then.'

David, feeling like a spare part, went and saw James out. *How dare Eve invite James to come with us? What about Robert and Alison?*

'Well, that went well, don't you think, David? Talk about killing two birds with one stone! James wants me to help him solve the murder, plus I'm going to get him the ideal woman!'

'What?' David exclaimed.

'Jane. She's crazy about James. We'll give her a lift as well.'

David shook his head, but he was relieved. At least Eve wasn't interested in James herself, as he feared. But why did she fancy herself as a matchmaker as well as an amateur sleuth? As far as he could see, James and Jane weren't at all suited. Couldn't Eve see that? Jane, despite having striking good looks, hadn't been spoilt or damaged by them and was a sweet, gentle girl, while James was a man of the world and thought too much of himself. This could only end in disaster. And why wouldn't Eve give up these silly notions of solving the murder? Had she forgotten what happened in the summer? No, he didn't think she had; but what she could recall were the exciting parts, not the dangerous and life-threatening ones. What was he going to do with her?

* * *

The following day Eve invited Jane to come over at five to start having her makeover. She knew it would take at least two hours, if not a little more.

Alison had said that she and Robert would travel into Chania that evening in Betty and Don's car, which had pleased her aunt no end. Betty was still smarting from the fact that Alison and Robert had decided to stay with Eve.

Eve was excited about the evening, thinking how well her plans were unfolding. To start with, James and Jane would be able to sit together in the back of David's car and chat during the journey into town. It would give them a little time to get to know each other.

David had told Alison and Robert about James's visit the previous evening, and they were both dismayed that he wanted Eve to help him find his aunt's killer. However, they were relieved to see that Eve seemed more interested in her role as a matchmaker at the moment. It was surely less ominous than being an amateur sleuth.

James was due at the house at seven thirty and they were all going to leave soon after. This should give them enough time to find parking spaces in Chania. While Eve was doing Jane's make-over, David popped back to his own house to get a few things. He was staying at Eve's for the whole of the Christmas period, a sort of trial run for marriage or living together, but he was in two minds about the experience. It had started off well and they had had a very romantic couple of days, but it was now turning out quite differently to what he had expected, mainly because of the murder hanging over them. David hadn't envisioned keeping such a close eye on Eve and he was finding it quite tiring.

Eve was definitely a high-maintenance woman. Because she got bored easily, she had to be entertained for most of the time. A quiet life did not suit Eve at all and David still wondered why she had come to live on the island of Crete after having led such a hectic life as a showbiz agent in London. Of course he was glad she had, otherwise he would never have met her.

However, when Eve was bored, she could be difficult to be with and his work as an author often suffered; but when she enjoyed life, she was the most exciting woman in the world. She really was too young to retire and he wondered what she was going to do with the rest of her life. She was well-off enough to never have to work again, but David thought this would drive her crazy. Eve had been stimulated in the summer by the murders and she hadn't been too fed up with the Christmas festivities, but without this murder to occupy her mind, David knew Eve would go stir-crazy before long. Perhaps this was why she had decided to try a bit of matchmaking. However, David didn't want to have to rely on murders or matchmaking to keep Eve occupied. Both were risky and one was certainly dangerous.

The doorbell rang dead on seven thirty and Alison went to let James in. 'Good evening, James. Eve and Jane are still upstairs getting ready I'm afraid, but David should be back from his own house in a moment.'

'It's Alison, isn't it — Betty's niece?'

'Yes, it is. Would you like a drink, James?'

'No, thank you. I imagine we'll be going soon,' James replied courteously.

David opened the front door and came in. 'James, good evening. No Eve yet? Not surprising! She always takes her time getting ready.'

However, Eve and Jane suddenly appeared at the top of the stairs. Eve looked as amazing as she always did, but all eyes were drawn towards Jane. She was absolutely stunning this evening.

Looking at herself in the mirror a few minutes previously, Jane couldn't believe her eyes. Eve had done a magnificent job, and out of nowhere the ugly duckling had turned into a beautiful swan. Jane had gained the confidence she much needed and she knew she wasn't going to fade into the background this evening.

Eve had washed and conditioned Jane's hair and it shone beautifully. Her long, straight black hair now fell in waves over her pure white shoulders. Jane's make-up was perfect; her baby-blue eyes were highlighted by sapphire-blue eye shadow and her lips were painted a luscious red. Eve had lent her a short midnight-blue dress, and because the two women were about the same size, it fitted perfectly. Jane had been a little nervous about wearing it, as she rarely exposed her body this much, usually wearing knee-length skirts and dresses. However, Eve thought she could get away with it as, like her, Jane was very slim.

Eve glanced at James and smiled to

herself. His eyes were glued to Jane. *Thank goodness. Perhaps David won't be jealous now. Though it was quite fun for a while!*

Eve enjoyed making David jealous, but it wasn't her best idea. David had nearly walked away from her a couple of times because he thought she was interested in someone else. However, for Eve it was only harmless fun and she most definitely wasn't keen on anybody but David.

Alison nudged Robert. His mouth was open and his eyes were fixed on Jane. He whispered apologies to Alison immediately.

'Well, this won't do at all,' Eve said. 'We're going to be late. I'm surprised Betty and Don haven't arrived yet.'

'Yes,' Robert agreed just as the doorbell rang.

David went and let Betty and Don in. Betty stared at Jane in amazement, but couldn't keep her mouth shut. 'Goodness, what have you done to yourself, girl? A bit over the top, isn't it?'

Jane felt as if she was about to burst into tears and Eve opened her mouth to have a go at Betty, when James piped up: 'Mrs Jones, there is absolutely no reason for you to criticise Jane or to be so rude and judgemental. She's looking absolutely beautiful this evening and I'm proud to be her escort tonight.'

Eve tried to stop herself from laughing out loud. What a wonderful put-down. *Well done, James!* she said to herself.

Betty was flabbergasted. How could he speak to her like that? She was an important woman in the community and he was putting her down in front of so many people. How dare he, especially with Eve in the room?

Nobody else said anything, all of them feeling slightly awkward. Alison, although she knew how stroppy her aunt was and how unnecessary her comment to Jane had been, didn't like to see her humiliated and decided to end the situation quickly before Eve decided to get involved and it ended up in all-out war. 'Come on, Aunt Betty, Don, we'll be late for our booking. Let's get going.'

'Yes, we'd better,' Don agreed, relieved that Alison had defused the situation.

Betty turned without saying another word and left, with her husband and Alison and Robert following her.

When they had gone, James turned to Jane. 'Are you all right, Jane?'

'Yes, thank you. I thought I looked nice, but . . . '

'You look beautiful. Take no notice of that old prude.'

'We are a small community here, you know,' David said crossly. 'We don't need feuds. Betty speaks before she thinks and doesn't usually mean what she says. We have to live here. You don't.' He was getting fed up with James. The likes of him always tried to take over.

'I'm sorry,' James said. 'But the woman insulted Jane.'

'Oh for goodness sake, let's forget about Betty,' Eve put in. 'She's a nasty piece of work, full stop. She's jealous of you, Jane, because you're young and beautiful. She's jealous of me as well and doesn't think I'm good enough for David. You have to ignore her. I know it's hard because you're sensitive, but you'll have to try. We all think you look lovely and that's all that matters. Nobody takes any notice of that dried up old prune. Anyway, it's time to go, so let's get a move on!'

Jane smiled. She was feeling better already. Eve was right about Betty, and she shouldn't worry about her. James found her attractive and that was what counted. He had barely looked at her before, but today he couldn't keep his eyes off her. To top it all, he had stood up for her against Betty. This was going to be a wonderful evening. She was sure of it.

* * *

Jane and James sat in the back seats of the car while David drove, with Eve in the seat next to him. Eve chatted about Betty continually and then realised she should be leaving the two lovebirds to talk to each other, so she started rambling on to David about his book. He, however, wished she'd be quiet as he hated being disturbed while driving. She knew this, but chose to forget it most of the time.

In the end, Eve started to eavesdrop on the conversation coming from the back of the car. Jane was asking James about his work as a merchant banker and she told him about her job as a social worker. Then the conversation drifted to his aunt.

'When was the last time you saw her, James?'

'At my mother's funeral last year.'

'Oh, I'm so sorry. How awful, losing both your mother and aunt in such a short period of time.'

'Well, it was difficult losing my mother — she died of cancer. We had always been close. But Jennifer . . . that was a different matter. She wasn't a nice woman at all. She couldn't even be bothered to go and see my mother when she was ill. I was surprised to see her at the funeral.'

'How terrible. Didn't they get on?'

'My mother was always trying to get in touch, inviting her over and so on, but Jennifer never wanted to know. I have no idea why. She was never kind to me either.'

'Yet you're desperate to find out who killed her?'

'Of course I am. I want to know why, Jane. There must have been some reason. She wasn't a thoughtful or loving person, but she must have done something completely evil for someone to want to murder her. I have to find out what it was.'

The car stopped and David parked up. Jane was sorry that the conversation had come to an end. It was interesting hearing about Jennifer Anderson, but more important, she was enjoying talking to James.

'Here we are,' Eve said. 'It's just a

little walk to the restaurant.'

Eve and David walked ahead, with James and Jane strolling a little way behind them. Eve pulled David closer as they walked.

'Did you hear their conversation in the car, darling?' she whispered.

'Of course not. I don't eavesdrop,' David replied adamantly.

Eve grunted, but carried on. 'James could be the killer!'

'What? Are you crazy?'

'Of course I'm not,' Eve said crossly. 'James told Jane he hated his aunt. Jennifer didn't even visit her sister when she was dying of cancer. How terrible is that? And he said Jennifer wasn't nice to him, but he didn't elaborate. What if he was here on Christmas Eve and gave the dessert wine to her as a Christmas present? He could have easily left on that day and then he could have come back on Boxing Day. I don't think he's short of money. The planes were running between here and London on both days, so it's entirely possible. Mark my words, he's a suspect; in fact, he may be the only suspect I've got.

* * *

Entering the restaurant, they found they were the last to arrive. Annie and Pete were already settled with pre-dinner drinks, and they smiled broadly when they saw Eve and David. It looked like Betty, Don, Alison and Robert had only got there a minute or so previously, as they were trying to decide where to sit. Not surprisingly, Betty made a profound effort to ignore the new arrivals. Ken and Jan had closed the Black Cat for the evening, so were there on a rare evening out. The final people attending the meal were Kevin and Lucy Fowler and Kevin's brother, Paul.

James hadn't met any of the Fowlers yet, and while Jane hadn't spoken to Kevin or Lucy, she had briefly had a few words with Paul before Christmas. She had walked past a garden he was working in, and thinking him rather good-looking, had stopped to ask directions to the local shop. She had thought herself rather brave talking to a strange man, but unfortunately she had been busy cleaning and looked a mess, and Paul hadn't been interested in engaging in a long conversation with her. This evening he didn't recognise her initially, but then it clicked who she was.

Damn. If I'd known she spruced up like this, I wouldn't have said so little to her. She probably remembers me being rude to her. I'll say I was busy and didn't have the time to talk. And I'll apologise. That's it. That's what I'll do.

Paul got up and walked towards Jane. 'Good evening,' he said. 'Jane isn't it? Lovely to see you again. Would you do me the great honour of sitting next to me?'

'I'm afraid she can't,' James said immediately. 'Jane is with me this evening. I would have thought it quite obvious by the fact that she's holding on to my arm.'

Pompous twit, Paul thought, scowling.

Jane was delighted that James had spoken up so quickly. She was finding it quite enjoyable to be fought over by two good-looking men for a change. Mind you, she was angry with Paul. He had shown no interest in her the other day when she wasn't looking her best, and he had been very offhand. Now that she had had a make-over and was looking attractive, he seemed keen to get to know her. *How superficial can you get?* she thought. She had forgotten, or perhaps refused to acknowledge, that James had also shown more interest in her after her make-over.

David, meanwhile, was getting worried that another awkward situation was arising. He was already apprehensive about Betty and Eve being in public together, especially in a restaurant of this calibre. Betty and James had also had a little set-to earlier on, and now James and Paul looked ready for a fight. How many people were going to have to be kept apart this evening?

For once it was Eve who calmed down the situation. 'You can have the pleasure of my company tonight, Paul,' she said and plonked herself down in the seat next to him. She didn't want to sit next to Paul, but like David, she didn't want arguments and tension in the restaurant that evening. However, she herself was feeling tense, knowing she was going to have to warn Jane that there was a possibility that James was the killer. It was a pity she hadn't known this before. Then she would never have given Jane the make-over and James wouldn't have been interested in her. Poor Jane. She was definitely in for heartbreak.

* * *

The evening started off pleasantly enough, although Eve did have to fend off Paul's attentions every now and again. However, a sharp glance from David usually put him off.

Even though she knew she was being a bit of a snob, Eve thought the restaurant wasn't the type of place Paul usually frequented, imagining he was the type who went out for pub meals back in England and here in Crete went to cheap local tavernas. Eve loved this restaurant, but preferred to go with David or a couple of her closest friends. To tell the truth, she was actually looking forward to the end of the evening and going home.

'So, how's the detecting going, Eve?' Betty boomed a little later in the evening, disturbing the peace and serenity of everyone enjoying their main course.

David and Robert both cringed, knowing that there would be some sort of confrontation now. What was Eve going to say? She would never admit that she wasn't any further forward, not to Betty anyway.

'Well, Betty,' Eve replied smugly, 'believe it or not, I have had a breakthrough — just today in fact. And I do have a suspect.' Eve knew she shouldn't have admitted this. It could frighten the killer and he or she might try and do away with her, but she couldn't help herself. She had to have one up on Betty.

There were gasps around the table and a couple of people asked who she thought it was. 'I'm afraid I can't say until I have more proof. I'm sure you can understand this. It would be awful if I went to the police with the wrong suspect, wouldn't it?'

'You are a foolish woman, Eve!' Betty shouted. 'You're putting your life in danger again. The killer could be at this table and may be planning his or her next murder . . . and that person might be you!'

'I'm not afraid,' Eve replied, trying to act calm. 'Phyllis failed miserably to kill me in the summer, so why should this killer have better luck? Anyway, if someone does try to kill me, it will be one of you at this table, won't it? The police won't have to go far to find their murderer.'

Betty shook her head while David

watched Eve take centre stage and revel in the attention she was getting. Her evidence was flimsy at best, and he couldn't understand why she had told so many people. This could very easily cost her her life. It didn't bear thinking about. He wished she hadn't made this announcement and would give up her stupid pursuit for the murderer, but he knew she wouldn't. He'd have to keep an extra-close eye on her from now on.

David, too, wanted the evening to end, knowing it had turned out to be pretty much a disaster. Too many people were having feuds, Eve had told them she suspected someone of the murder, Paul was flirting with her, Jane was being courted by a possible murderer; and to top it all, they were paying a fortune for a meal he'd normally love, but wasn't enjoying one bit. Could life get any worse?

8

The following day Eve and David went to the Black Cat around one, where they had arranged to meet Jane. She wanted to buy them lunch to thank Eve for her make-over. 'I'm going to tell Jane what I think about James,' Eve said as they strolled down to the bar. She wasn't looking forward to doing this at all and was feeling pretty nervous. On top of this, she had a bit of a headache after the previous night, but she said it was due to Betty's loud voice and not the alcohol.

'You're not sure about James being the killer, so don't say anything, Eve. In fact, as much as I don't like the guy, I think it's highly unlikely that he did murder his aunt. Yes, he probably inherits her house, but nobody has admitted seeing him here on Christmas Eve, have they? It would be very difficult to get around without being noticed.'

'I know nobody's said they saw him, but he could have been very careful.'

'Well, even if he is the murderer, I hardly think he's going to kill Jane, do you? He probably had a motive to kill his aunt, but I can't see a reason for him to do away with Jane. He seems to like her.'

'But David, I don't want her to spend the rest of her life with a killer. He could get away with murdering his aunt and later marry Jane. Then one day she'll upset him and he'll try and kill her. It's better we do something now.'

'Eve, they hardly know each other. Who says they're even going to get serious, let alone get married? Please, Eve, don't say anything yet. Not until you have more proof.'

'All right. I won't say anything today, but I'll keep a close eye on both of them. And if I suspect he's up to no good, I'll be in there like a rocket.'

'Okay, okay,' David agreed to keep

the peace, but he still doubted that James had killed his aunt. 'Look, here comes Jane. Be quiet about James . . . Jane, lovely to see you. Now, what can I get you to drink? Eve's back on the G and Ts.'

'Oh, a white wine please. But put it all on my tab. This lunch is on me, David.'

'That's so kind of you, Jane,' Eve gushed. 'Although it's quite unnecessary. I loved doing your make-over.'

'Please, I really want to do this.'

David gave Eve a look which told her to shut up and be gracious. To David's relief, she did as he asked for once.

'Well, thank you very much, Jane. It's very kind of you,' Eve said.

Jane sat down and Eve noticed she was glowing. She had done her make-up on her own today, but had taken Eve's advice and she looked gorgeous. However, Eve thought the glow was more likely from her feelings for James. She shuddered. What had she started? She hoped she was completely wrong and James wasn't the murderer.

'Oh, Eve, thank you so much for helping me with my look yesterday. It's given me so much confidence. I learnt such a lot from you as well. I think I know how to make the best of my features now.' She paused, pleased to see Eve looking gratified, and then she smiled broadly. 'And James — what a wonderful man. I had the best evening with him. I can't believe that he's interested in me.'

Eve had to stop herself from blurting out that he could be a cold-blooded killer.

'When you dropped us off at my dad's house yesterday, he was such a gentleman. He didn't presume anything. He just kissed me before walking back to his hotel, but what a kiss. Oh, Eve, it was both passionate and tender at the same time. I think I'm falling in love with him already.'

'That's fantastic,' Eve said, trying to look happy for her new friend. 'But try and take it slowly. You don't know him that well yet, so don't rush into things.'

Jane nodded, but Eve could see her mind was far away, thinking of James. There was no way that Jane would be able to put the brakes on this relationship.

No more eavesdropping for me, thought Eve. *All I do is hear things I'd rather not know about*.

David came back with the drinks and they studied the menu and ordered lunch. A little later, when Jane went to the ladies', Eve frantically told David what Jane had confided in her about her feelings for James. Eve didn't feel as if she could keep this from David.

'This is terrible, David. I could have put her life in danger.'

'Oh, shush, Eve. You have absolutely no evidence that James is the killer apart from the fact that he didn't like his aunt. I think you need more than that. I mean, James wasn't even in the country on Christmas Eve.'

'That's what he says. I've already told you there were planes out of Crete on

Christmas Eve and planes back in on Boxing Day. We've been through this already. I bet the police haven't even checked the airline records.' She was getting frustrated with David. Didn't he ever listen to her?

'Why don't you tell Dimitris Kastrinakis then?'

'What? And let him have all the glory?'

'I don't think you'll be allowed to check plane records, Eve. Only the police will be able to do that. And does it matter who gets the glory? If James is the killer, isn't it better that he's caught, whoever gets him?'

Eve grunted. It did matter to her. She wanted to be the one who was on television being congratulated after discovering and capturing Jennifer's killer. However, she wasn't able to tell David this, as she saw Jane coming back to the table. It was probably for the best, as David didn't appreciate the big-headed side of her personality.

David steered the rest of the

conversation away from the murder, but he had great difficulty in keeping the ladies entertained. Jane seemed miles away, no doubt thinking about James, and Eve wasn't completely concentrating either. She was thinking of the best way to prove that James was the murderer without getting the police involved.

As they were finishing their food, Annie and Pete came into the bar, with Alison and Robert following behind them. Eve's house guests had borrowed Eve's car and gone for a drive inland that morning, eager to get away from talk of the murder. Robert was determined not to get involved. He still had nightmares of being in Eve's car when the brakes failed and he saw his life flash before him.

The two couples joined Eve, David and Jane at their table. Then Paul came in and asked to join the group. He hoped that as James wasn't there, he might have a chance to talk to Jane. They decided to have a kitty for the drinks, but as they were putting their money in, a deep voice broke the silence and Jane blushed.

'Can anyone join?' James asked, grinning.

'James,' Jane replied quickly, both blushing and smiling at the same time. 'Of course you can. We're just putting together a kitty for the drinks.'

James got his money out and pulled up a chair, putting it next to Jane. Paul's heart sank. Was he never going to get a chance with her? She seemed to only have eyes for that poser.

'Right,' Pete said, 'who's going up first?'

'Not me,' Eve said, butting in. 'That awful Yiannis is at the bar. I don't want to talk to him. We always argue when we bump into each other.'

'Well, I think the men should go up in turn,' James said. 'But first let's all write down what we want. I'm sure that will make it easier for the person going to the bar.'

Pompous twat, thought Paul. *Always trying to take over*.

David, Pete and Paul decided to have

lagers; James wanted whisky; and Annie and Jane were drinking wine. Eve decided to stick to gin and tonics.

The afternoon passed pleasantly enough for everyone, apart from Paul, who felt depressed as he watched James and Jane locked in conversation for most of the time. They seemed to be in a world of their own, not joining in with the others, but nobody apart from Paul seemed to mind. Eventually he started chatting with everyone else. The conversation drifted from sport to food to Betty; but despite efforts from Eve, everybody avoided talking about the murder.

* * *

'Who's for another drink, then?' David asked later in the afternoon, hoping that they didn't. They had already had quite a few and he felt like a lie-down.

'I feel nauseous,' Eve said.

'We'd better get you home then,' David said. 'I don't know; too many gin and tonics today, I think.'

'No,' Eve continued. 'I can handle my drink, thank you very much. I feel like I did when I had arsenic poisoning back in the summer.'

'Oh come on, Eve, you're imagining it,' David said, not thinking that anyone would have the audacity to poison her yet again with the same poison.

Eve tried to get up, but she struggled and then felt the room spinning around her.

'Oh no, not aga . . . '

* * *

When Eve woke up, she was lying in a hospital bed. She still felt sick and her head was throbbing.

'Eve,' David spoke angrily, 'I knew this would happen. Why did you have to start again, why?' He was angry and she had no idea what she had done wrong.

'David, don't shout at Eve; she's not well and needs to rest,' Annie said gently, hoping he'd calm down.

'I'm not really cross, Annie; you know I'm not. I'm only concerned about Eve.'

Annie gave David a hug. He looked so forlorn, and she did know deep down that he was desperately worried about losing Eve.

Eve looked around the room and it suddenly dawned on her that she was in hospital again. She groaned inwardly. This was the one place she didn't want to be.

There was an elderly Greek woman in the bed opposite and a younger one in the bed next to her. Around her bed were David, Annie, Pete, Jane and James. Paul was standing a few feet away. She remembered that you could have as many visitors as you wanted in Chania hospital and she was pleased that so many people had come to see her. However, although she was trying her hardest, she couldn't remember what had happened and why she was in hospital. She vaguely recalled having lunch with David and Jane, but that was all. She couldn't remember anything else.

'David, what happened? Why am I here?'

'You mean you can't remember?'

'No, I can't. All I remember is having lunch with you and Jane, and that's it. What's wrong with me? Why am I in hospital?'

David's heart softened. He knew he should be angry with her, but she hadn't done a lot of snooping yet. All she was guilty of was suspecting James of being the killer, and she hadn't told anyone apart from him. Her reputation had preceded her and the murderer must have wanted her out of the way, knowing how good she was as an amateur detective. Then David suddenly remembered the previous evening. At the restaurant Eve had foolishly announced that she had a suspect. If she had indeed been poisoned again, it must have been somebody who had been there.

'Eve, darling, you were feeling nauseous in the pub and then you collapsed. You said you felt the same as you had when you were poisoned in the summer. We don't know yet, but the doctors are doing tests to see if they can find arsenic in your system.'

'Oh my God,' Eve exclaimed. 'I haven't accused anyone of killing Jennifer yet, but the murderer is already trying to get rid of me. David, I'm scared.' She was almost in tears.

'Shush, darling. It'll be all right.' But as he said it, David wasn't convinced, and nor were Annie or David. James and Jane stood at the side awkwardly.

'I feel terrible,' James finally said. 'I asked you to try and find my aunt's killer, and now you're in hospital and could have died.'

'Don't worry about it, James,' Eve muttered, feeling exhausted. 'I haven't really done anything yet, so the murderer would have struck anyway.'

Then the truth hit her as her memory started coming back. James was her number-one suspect. In fact he was her only suspect, and he was standing in front of her as bold as brass. And to top it all, she had stupidly announced at the restaurant the previous evening that she had a suspect. All to get one up on that woman, Betty. Suddenly she felt sick again and wished they would all leave, all of them apart from David of course.

'Are you all right, darling?' David asked. 'You look as if you're going to be sick again.'

'I thought I was, but I'm all right now.'

'You poor thing,' Annie said. 'I bet you never thought you'd be in hospital so soon again.'

'I hoped I'd never be in hospital in Crete ever again. I hope I don't miss the New Year's Eve celebrations. I was looking forward to them so much.'

'I'm sure they won't keep you in long,' Pete added. 'It was only a night last time, wasn't it?'

Eve nodded as Dimitris Kastrinakis and another police officer entered the ward. 'I told you, Miss Masters, to keep your nose out of the murder,' he said sternly.

‘I’ve hardly done anything at all,’ Eve wailed. ‘Hardly anything. The killer wanted to stop me before I even started. I’m sure of it.’

‘She really hasn’t done much,’ David agreed. ‘We don’t know yet if she has been poisoned; but if she has, the person who did it wanted her out of the way even before she started gathering evidence.’

‘Well, Miss Masters,’ Dimitris continued, ‘I see your reputation precedes you.’

Eve tried to force a smile, but was thinking that if the murderer was going to try and eliminate her anyway, she might as well try and hunt him out.

‘What a crowd you have around your bed. You are a popular woman, Miss Masters,’ the doctor said, entering the ward.

Everyone turned and Eve wondered if he had the results. If he had, it would be a lot quicker than last time.

‘I have the results of your tests, Miss Masters,’ the doctor continued.

Eve's heart started racing. In a way she hoped it wasn't poison. It was a tad scary to know that someone wanted to kill you again. However, she felt a rush of adrenaline. Life was getting exciting again.

'I am afraid we have found arsenic in your sample. I believe that it was found in your sample in the summer?'

'Yes, yes it was,' she said hurriedly. 'Oh my goodness, someone is trying to kill me again.'

Eve looked full of life and excited. David sighed. She shouldn't be feeling like this. Someone had tried to kill her; Eve should be scared, not exhilarated. He also noticed that Dimitris was frowning.

'I need to speak to Miss Masters alone, so could you all wait outside please.'

'We'll be off home now, if that's all right,' Alison said. 'Shall we feed Portia for you? I expect David will be staying for a while?' She knew how much Eve worried about her dog.

'Oh yes, please. Oh dear, what about dinner? I don't suppose I'll be home.'

'Don't worry about us,' Robert said. 'We'll pop out somewhere for a bite. You take care. This should be a warning, Eve. No more searching for killers.'

'He's right, Eve. Get lots of rest and forget about murders and suchlike,' Annie said, giving Eve a kiss on the cheek.

'I'll take Jane home,' James said. 'I think I can make my way back from the hospital, as it's so close to the highway.'

'You can follow us if you like,' Annie said.

'Thanks; will do.'

As they all left, Paul stood there looking awkward and alone, and then said his goodbyes and went. Dimitris stood talking to another police officer for a few minutes.

'I don't know why I thought Paul was creepy,' Eve said. 'He's really quite a sad, lonely guy. Oh, why couldn't Jane have liked him? Instead she's getting a lift home with a crazed killer.'

'Eve, you do change your mind about people. You couldn't stand Paul before; and anyway, we have no proof James is the killer,' David said, exasperated.

'How did everybody get here?' Eve asked, changing the subject while trying to make sense of the afternoon. 'There were so many of you. Did you get an ambulance?'

'No, we thought it would be quicker to bring you here, so you came in my car with Alison. Pete and Annie took Robert and Paul in theirs and James and Jane followed in his car. I have no idea how Paul is getting home. I doubt if James will want him in his car, but perhaps there's room in Pete's.'

'Right, Miss Masters,' Dimitris said, 'what have you been up to?'

'Nothing, absolutely nothing,' she replied indignantly. 'I have one suspect and I've told David here who it is, but I only decided on him last night, and I've done nothing about it, and he doesn't know I suspect him. In fact I gave him a helping hand in the romance department — that is, before I thought he was a murderer. And now this beautiful innocent girl is in love with him, and she could be his next victim. What have I done?' She burst into tears and David rushed to comfort her.

'There, there, darling. It'll be all right,' he said, trying to console her.

Dimitris stood still, feeling embarrassed. He never knew what to do when women cried. It was hardly her fault. If the girl had been attracted to that man, she would probably have managed to get a date with him anyway, so Eve shouldn't blame herself. She was probably in shock.

When Eve's tears had subsided, Dimitris continued talking. 'Could you tell me who this suspect is?'

'James, Jennifer's nephew,' Eve mumbled, a few tears still falling.

Dimitris was surprised. 'James!' He exclaimed. 'He didn't come to the island until the twenty-sixth of December.'

'There was nothing stopping him

leaving on the twenty-fourth and returning on the twenty-sixth, was there?' Eve asked. 'He's a rich man. Have you checked with the airlines?'

'We haven't, but before we do that, can you tell us why you think he killed his aunt?'

'Last night a group of us went into Chania for a meal, and we took James and Jane in the car with us. I heard him tell Jane how much he hated his aunt, particularly because she had been horrible to his mother, even refusing to see her when she had cancer.'

'I believe he was with you in the Black Cat this afternoon?'

'Yes he was, and so is definitely a suspect. The men went to get the drinks in turn. I reckon the arsenic was in my drink like last time, don't you?'

'It's highly probable, Miss Masters. Now, can you give me the names of whoever could have touched your drink, please?' Dimitris asked, indicating to the other officer to take out his notebook.

'Well, as I said, there was James Anderson . . . '

'He had the same name as his aunt?'

'This afternoon I overheard him tell Jane he was born out of wedlock. Another reason Jennifer despised her sister . . . and him. It seems she was quite a prude. Oh, this is good; I'm getting my memory back. I felt quite confused when I woke up.'

And you keep talking and talking, Dimitris thought. *Poor David*.

'Anyway, back to the drinks. David went to get a round in, but of course he's not the murderer.' However, she saw the police officer write his name down.

'What is your last name, sir?' he asked.

'Baker.'

Eve frowned. How could they possibly think her darling David was a killer? He would never poison her.

'Anyway,' she said severely, 'then there was Pete Davies and Paul Fowler. Ken Stewart served at the bar. Jan was in the kitchen all afternoon, as they were very busy serving food. Oh, I nearly forgot — that Yiannis Neonakis was at the bar all afternoon. He could easily have slipped something in my drink. I wouldn't put it past him.'

'Now, now, Miss Masters,' Dimitris said harshly. 'We won't have any of that. There was enough of a feud going on between you two last summer, and he was innocent.'

'Humph,' was all Eve could say.

'Eve did announce at dinner in Chania last night that she had a suspect,' David added.

'Ah, now you tell me,' Dimitris said. 'She didn't do completely *nothing* then. Were any of these people here today?'

'Yes,' Eve continued, slightly annoyed with David for mentioning that she wasn't quite as innocent as she had made herself out to be. 'James and Jane, David of course, Annie and Pete, Ken and Jan Stewart and Paul Fowler. Apart from that, Betty and Don Jones were there, and Kevin and Lucy Fowler.'

'Right, we shall question everybody and search the houses, but it is doubtful we shall find anything again. You take care, Miss Masters, and no snooping. I mean it.' Dimitris sounded severe, but Eve took no notice.

'Remember to check the airline seat lists for Christmas Eve,' was Eve's last remark.

Dimitris turned and gave her a stern look.

'You are going to push that man too far, Eve, you really are,' David said when Dimitris had left.

'Well, if I hadn't given him that idea, he'd never have thought of it himself, would he?'

David shook his head. There was never a dull moment with Eve, but in reality he was worried. She actually hadn't done much to find the murderer, and he or she had already tried to get rid of her. Her life truly was in danger, and from now on he was going to watch her like a hawk. He wasn't going to let her out of his sight if he could help it, but he knew that Eve wouldn't let him hang on to her like a puppy. He was going to have to be very devious. Why did Christmas have to turn out to be so complicated?

9

James sped out of the hospital grounds. In his mirror he could see Paul frantically waving behind them, but there was no way he was going to give him a lift home. James was relieved that Jane was oblivious to Paul's presence. He was certain she was far too nice to leave him stranded.

James gave the impression that he was a secure person, not to mention a sophisticated and debonair man. Yes, he had a high-powered job and money, but truth be told, women confused him. He had discovered that they never seemed to say what they meant and kept changing their minds. His relationships had been short-lived and he didn't want this pattern to continue. Most certainly he didn't want to fight Paul for Jane. Perhaps it was because he wanted to concentrate on romancing her without any distractions, or maybe it was because he was afraid of losing. He had enough to cope with at the moment with the police hovering around all the time. He was also trying to arrange to take Jennifer's body back to England to be buried, but at the moment it still hadn't been released and he was getting anxious.

'I do hope Eve's going to be all right,' Jane said, interrupting his thoughts. 'What an awful thing to happen. She's barely started looking for the killer and he's already tried to get rid of her.'

'Well, it goes to show what a good detective she must be. If the killer was here in the summer, he or she would have already known that. If not, her reputation certainly did precede her.'

'Well, I hope she stops all this nonsense. I like her and it's not often I make new friends. I wouldn't like this friendship to be cut short.'

'I wouldn't have thought you two would have got on so well. You're like chalk and cheese.'

'I know, but in the little time I've

known her, she's given me confidence in myself. I am a bit worried though. I hope she doesn't find me boring. I'm sure she must have worked with all sorts of exciting people back in England when she was in show business.'

'You're not boring in the least, my darling. Don't put yourself down. I for one am delighted to have met you.'

Jane sighed with pleasure. Life had certainly taken a turn for the better.

* * *

Half an hour later, Jane and James were sitting on the settee in Jennifer's home. That morning, the police had given James permission to use her house. They had searched it thoroughly and had found nothing which gave any clues as to who the killer might be.

'You're sure you don't find this strange? Being in my aunt's house, I mean,' he asked.

'Not at all,' she replied. 'After all, I am staying in my dad's house and he's dead too.'

'I'm glad you're okay with it. It doesn't worry me at all, but I know you're sensitive. I thought it would be more comfortable than my hotel.' He went and poured them both whiskies.

'I wonder how hard it will be to sell both our houses,' Jane said.

'I would imagine it will be pretty difficult,' he replied. 'A lot of people wouldn't like to live in a house where a murder's been committed, but then I expect some would find an eerie and ghoulish quality about it.' He smiled at Jane. She looked vulnerable and younger than she was, and as much as he wanted her now, he knew he had to take things slowly with her. He reckoned she was quite innocent and could be frightened off if he came on too strong.

He stroked her cheek and she smiled at him. Touching her lips with his, he kissed her gently and she felt a warm glow spread through her body. She wanted more, but it seemed inappropriate in Jennifer's house. She also had to admit that she felt a little on edge being alone with him. She had only just met James and hardly knew anything about him.

The two of them cuddled up together on the settee saying nothing, yet feeling comfortable with each other. It had been a long day and both started to drift off, when they were startled by a knock at the door.

'Who on earth can that be?' Jane asked, feeling slightly apprehensive.

'I have no idea. Nobody would know we're here, but I suppose I'd better go and see who it is.'

Jane was nervous as James went and answered the front door. A few moments later he came back with Dimitris Kastrinakis, the police officer in charge of his aunt's murder, and two other police officers.

Jane sat up. 'What's wrong?' she asked. 'I hope nothing's happened to Eve?'

'No, Miss Masters will be fine. It's Mr Anderson I must speak to, in private.'

'Anything you have to say, you can say in front of Jane.'

'Very well. We have heard that you did not like your aunt.'

'Who told you that?' James asked sharply. 'The only person I've mentioned it to is Jane.' He turned to her and asked, 'Did you tell the police?' He sounded angry, and Jane felt she was about to burst into tears.

'Of course not, James,' she mumbled.

'Oh, I'm sorry, darling. I know you would never do anything to hurt me. What am I thinking?' He went over and hugged her and Jane felt relieved. He was probably shocked by the arrival of Dimitris, not to mention a little nervous. That was all. However, she wondered what was going on.

Is James a suspect in his aunt's murder? No, it can't be so! Not my handsome, intelligent James, the man I was hoping to build a future with. The man I was dreaming of marrying last night when I was lying alone in bed. No, he's not a cold-blooded killer. I don't believe it, I don't.

'I'm afraid we can't reveal our source, Mr Anderson, but rest assured it wasn't Miss Phillips here.'

James's face suddenly lit up. 'I know exactly who it was. It was that woman in hospital. Eve Masters! I told Jane about my dislike for my aunt in the car going into Chania. She was obviously eavesdropping. It could have been David of course, but I very much doubt it. He's not interested in anyone's business and was concentrating on driving. Anyway, how could I have poisoned her? I wasn't here. I didn't arrive on Crete until the twenty-sixth of December. I have the ticket to prove it.'

'We have been in touch with the airline, sir, and have discovered that you were a passenger on the last flights from Chania to Athens and Athens to Heathrow on December the twenty-fourth. I am afraid I am going to have to arrest you on suspicion of murdering your aunt Jennifer Anderson.'

Before Dimitris could say anything

else, Jane let out a scream and then fainted.

* * *

Half an hour later, Jane woke up on Jennifer's settee. She looked around and couldn't see James or Dimitris. However, Annie was sitting at the table reading a magazine.

Jane sat up slowly, her head hurting badly. 'Annie, where's James?'

Annie jumped. 'Oh, Jane, you're awake. You don't remember what happened?'

'Yes, I do. I hoped it was a dream, but I can see that it wasn't. James has been arrested for murdering his aunt, hasn't he?'

'I'm afraid so.'

'I don't believe he did it, Annie. He didn't like his aunt, but I can't see him killing her.'

'None of us knew him that well, so we don't know what he's really like, Jane. I know you've spent more time than us with him, but it still wasn't that long.'

Jane had started sobbing and she tried to wipe the tears away, but they kept coming. Before long she was crying uncontrollably.

'There, there, dear,' Annie, said, moving over to the settee and putting her arms around Jane, hoping to console her. 'Hopefully the police are wrong. I mean, just because he was here on Christmas Eve, doesn't mean he was the one who killed his aunt. All I'm worried about is that he didn't tell anyone he was here before Christmas. It does make him look guilty even if he's not.'

'I hate Eve,' Jane said vehemently. 'It's all her fault. If it wasn't for her, James would be here with me.'

Oh dear, thought Annie. *Eve's gone and done it again. She's made another enemy*. 'She must have had your best interests at heart. She went to a lot of trouble to make you look attractive for James, so she must now think you are in danger.'

'Humph,' was all Jane said.

'Anyway, if you're feeling better, I'll

give you a lift home. I'm sure you don't want to stay here.'

'Thank you, thank you very much. I don't fancy walking home.'

10

The following day the whole village was alive with gossip about James and his arrest. Most people were shocked. They had found him to be a polite and sophisticated man and it was hard to believe that he was capable of murder.

Annie had told her husband the news after she had taken Jane home. Pete had been out when Dimitris Kastrinakis had called to ask Annie for her help with Jane.

Annie asked Pete not to mention to anyone that Eve was the one who had suggested to the police that James was the killer. However, he had let it slip to Robert and Robert, never being one who was good at keeping a secret, had mentioned it a couple times around the village, and soon everybody in the area knew.

'Trust Eve to get involved again,'

Betty commented to Kevin Fowler in the local shop. 'Serves her right that she ended up being poisoned. The police warned her not to interfere, but would she listen?'

'From what I gather, she did very little interfering,' Kevin replied sharply. 'The killer, if it really is James, wanted her out of the way from the start. He or she obviously reckons that Eve is a good detective. And nobody deserves to be poisoned. Eve could have died, you know.'

Kevin wasn't keen on Betty. He thought she was overbearing and he didn't like the way she tried to control everybody. He and his wife, Lucy, tried to avoid most of the activities she organised.

'No point being good at anything if you're dead,' Betty snapped and walked away.

Kevin shook his head. Betty was a most obnoxious woman.

* * *

Eve was sitting up in bed waiting for the doctor to come round and hopefully discharge her. She was bored. It was already midday and nobody had visited her yet. She was quite put out. After all, she had almost died again. Didn't anyone care?

David wasn't coming to the hospital until she was discharged and he could take her home. She was going to phone him when she got the good news. *Please let the news be positive*, she wished. *I couldn't bear to spend another night in hospital*.

Eve hated staying in communal rooms and had found it practically impossible to sleep. She needed her privacy and decided there and then that whatever happened, she would discharge herself.

She had closed her eyes, wishing the time away, when a voice called out, 'Eve, how are you?' She jumped and was surprised to see who her visitors were. They weren't particular friends of hers and she wondered why they had come.

'Kevin, Lucy, how lovely to see you. I'm not doing too badly, thank you,' she answered politely.

'It was quite a shock when my brother, Paul, told us what happened to you. Obviously we heard about the goings on in the summer, but we didn't think you'd be targeted again,' Kevin remarked.

'Nor did I,' Eve replied. 'Especially as I hadn't done much to try and find the killer. I was attempting to keep a low profile this time. The police warned me, but apparently the murderer thought I was a threat.'

'It looks like it,' Lucy said. 'And on top of that, we hear Jane is very upset with you.'

'With me!' Eve exclaimed. 'Why? What have I done? All I've done is help her.'

'Well, according to her it's your fault James has been arrested,' Lucy continued.

'James arrested! That's news to me,' Eve yelled, startling the old woman in the bed opposite.

'Oh, you don't know then?' Kevin asked. 'You told the police he hated his aunt and they found out he was here on Christmas Eve. The long and short of it is that he's their prime suspect in Jennifer's murder. They arrested him last night.'

'Oh my God,' Eve stuttered. 'So he must have flown out on Christmas Eve and come back on Boxing Day. I knew it. I told the police to check the plane records. At last they're taking me seriously . . . I didn't want to hurt Jane though. I knew she liked him and at first I thought he was okay. It was only when I heard how much he disliked his aunt that I became suspicious.'

Both Kevin and Lucy nodded. 'I'm afraid I don't think James is a very nice man,' Lucy said. 'He seems stuck up to me and not interested in us lowly folk. He's been quite rude to our Paul. He was a bit upset last night when they were here in the hospital. James rushed ahead with Jane and they got into his car, leaving Paul behind. Paul was sure James could see him waving, but he didn't stop and give him a lift home. I don't think there was any room in Annie and Pete's car, so Paul had to fork out for a taxi. No, that James is not a nice man.'

'Oh, I'm sorry about that,' Eve said. 'Paul should have waited a bit longer. David was only here for about another half an hour after the others left. I was so tired that I soon fell asleep, and David went off home. Oh well, I suppose I've made another enemy in Jane; but if it's true that James is the killer, she'll thank me in the end.'

'Hopefully,' Lucy said. 'But when you're in love . . . '

Eve felt quite upset. She wasn't looking forward to a confrontation with Jane.

'Anyway, we'd better be off,' Kevin said. 'We were on our way to Chania, but thought we'd pop in to see if you were okay. Is there anything we can get you?'

'No, I have everything I need. Thanks for coming to see me.'

As Kevin and Lucy left the ward, the doctor came in. 'Well, Miss Masters, you look brighter today. Just a couple more tests and then I'm sure we'll be able to send you home.'

'Thank goodness for that,' she replied.

However, it suddenly hit her that she wasn't looking forward to going home after all. David had been angry with her and would be watching her like a hawk, Jane now despised her, and Betty would be thinking that justice had been served with Eve being poisoned once again. To cap it all, months of boredom loomed ahead. Eve had hoped this murder might keep her occupied for some time, but it was all over before it had really begun.

* * *

While Eve was perched uncomfortably in her hospital bed, Jane Phillips was sitting in her front garden with a gin and tonic. She wondered if winter was ever going to come; it was such a lovely, sunny day and it didn't seem at all like December. She leant back in her deckchair, allowing the sun to warm her face.

It was only midday and there was more gin than tonic in her glass, but Jane didn't care. She didn't usually drink much, but today she needed it. She was still in shock after James had been arrested, but she hoped she'd be all right in a couple of days' time. After all, she hardly knew James and it couldn't have been love, could it? It had just been a silly crush, but then perhaps it could have developed into something more. James was so handsome and such a gentleman, and they had talked and talked at the pub the previous afternoon. She usually found it difficult to chat to men, but it had been easy with him. She couldn't believe he was guilty of the crime. James wasn't capable of murder. Just because he didn't like his aunt, didn't mean he had killed her.

Jane wasn't quite as angry with Eve today. Eve had put a lot of effort into getting her together with James, so she must have had cause to think he was the murderer. Anyway, she probably wouldn't have said anything to the police before talking to her first if she hadn't been poisoned. She had wanted to find the killer on her own and take the glory for herself. Whatever the truth was, she was going to have it out with Eve. She had liked her and didn't want the friendship to end before discussing the situation with her first.

Jane took a sip of her gin and tonic and then closed her eyes, remembering the first time James had seen her with her new look. She would never forget that moment. He had been totally mesmerised. Perhaps it would take her more than a couple of days to forget about him.

'Hello,' a voice interrupted her thoughts. 'Are you all right?'

Jane sat up and took off her

sunglasses. Paul stood there, looking quite bashful. She felt sorry for him, especially after the way he had been treated by James. James had pushed him to one side when he had tried to talk to her and she knew that James had avoided giving him a lift home from the hospital. However, she knew she was guilty as well. Although she had seen Paul waving, she hadn't wanted James to give him a lift, not wanting anyone to spoil their time alone together.

'I'm fine,' Jane said. 'Would you like a drink?'

'Yes, please. A beer would be great if you have one.'

'I do. Come in the garden and sit down.'

Paul was trembling as he pulled up a deckchair. So much for being one of the lads. He was actually quite shy and hadn't had a great deal of experience with women. There had been a few girlfriends, but they hadn't lasted long and he'd never been married or engaged. He always put on an air of confidence, but he was far from being self-assured.

'There you go,' Jane said, giving Paul his beer.

'Are you feeling okay, what with James being arrested?'

'Yes. I mean they haven't proved anything yet,' Jane said. 'Just because he was here on Christmas Eve doesn't mean he killed his aunt, does it? He obviously came here to see her before Christmas and then he came back after because she was murdered.'

Paul's heart sank. She wasn't convinced James was guilty. Perhaps there wasn't any hope for him. 'But it is pretty likely though, isn't it? He didn't tell anyone that he was here on Christmas Eve. That smacks of guilt.'

'But perhaps he didn't tell anyone because it would make him look guilty, not because he is guilty,' Jane said sharply. She was getting worked up. She knew Paul liked her so he was trying to convince her that James was guilty, but she couldn't switch off her feelings so quickly. It was turning out to be a difficult day. One minute she wondered if James was guilty, the next she felt the opposite. And now here was Paul trying to convince her that James was the murderer. The next thing he'd be doing would be asking her out. Did he think she would be able to start another relationship so soon? She wanted to talk to Eve. Her anger with her had more or less dissipated now. Eve was intuitive and would help her through this.

'What are you thinking about, Jane?' Paul asked after an awkward silence. 'You seem miles away.'

'Oh, I'm so sorry, Paul. My mind was drifting. I'm terrible company today.'

Paul was upset. How could he stop her thinking about James? Suddenly he had an idea. 'Look Jane, I know you like James and I'd be a fool to think otherwise, so let me just be a friend to you. Hopefully he'll be exonerated and be back in no time, but if not I'll be here to give you support, no strings attached.'

Jane studied Paul. Was he being sincere? She'd like to think so, but she doubted it. Still, she hated to have enemies, so she smiled at him. 'Thank you, Paul. It's very kind of you. We'll see how things go.' Seeing his face fall, she tried to make amends. 'Would you like another beer? It's so warm for the end of December. I'm sure you could do with one.'

'I'd love one,' Paul replied, cheering up instantly.

All was not lost yet.

* * *

Eve got up and went to answer the front door. She was pleased to be back home, even though David was upstairs carrying on with writing his second novel. He didn't want to be disturbed for the next few hours as he was behind schedule, and anyway he had told Eve that she needed to rest. She knew he was right, but she always found it difficult to keep still for long.

The following evening was New Year's Eve and they were going to Annie and Pete's party. Eve still didn't feel one hundred per cent, and she had to relax and recover from the poisoning so that she could cope with a late night. But she was bored, especially now that she didn't have the murder to keep her mind occupied. 'Who's that at the door?' she asked Portia, her dog.

Portia looked up at her, but seeing no food was on offer, went back to sleep again. The dog had been spoilt over the Christmas period and Eve thought she had better cut down on her treats after the holidays were over.

Eve finally got to the door and stood there in amazement when she opened it. 'James,' she said, dumbfounded.

'Well, it's not often you're almost lost for words, Eve. Feeling guilty, are we?'

'David is here, I'll have you know,' she replied hurriedly.

'Don't worry, Eve, I haven't come here to murder you. I just want to talk.'

'All right, come in.' She led James

into the sitting room. She felt slightly tense, wondering what was going on. 'Would you like a drink?' she asked, trying not to show that she was nervous.

'I wouldn't mind a whisky if you have one.'

'Yes, I do. I think I'll have a metaxa,' she replied.

As she got the drinks, she found she was trembling. This was crazy. It was highly unlikely that James had escaped from jail, so the police must have released him. She didn't have anything to worry about apart from James being angry with her, but she wished David was downstairs. He was probably so engrossed in his work that he hadn't even heard the doorbell ring.

'So the police have released you, James,' Eve said, handing him his drink.

'Well, I didn't break out of prison, Eve,' he said, with a mischievous grin on his face. 'You know, I should be very cross with you, turning me in as you did.'

'I didn't intend to tell the police I thought you might have killed your aunt, James. I was a little worried when I heard you say how much you disliked her. You seemed to be the only one with any motive to kill her, but I was only concerned for Jane. However, after I was poisoned, I had to tell the police what I heard you say. After all, I was nearly killed again.'

'Whoever did it didn't give you enough arsenic. It looked like a warning to me.'

'You seem very knowledgeable about poisons, James.'

'I know a little, but that doesn't make me a killer, nor does it mean I tried to kill you or my aunt. In fact, I have come here to swear to you that I did not kill my aunt or poison you.'

'And I'm supposed to believe that?'

'It's up to you, but I'm telling you the truth.'

Eve sat there for a moment before saying anything else. She had noticed that James hadn't elaborated on his knowledge of poisons, but she didn't think it worth questioning him. She was certain he wouldn't tell her anything else.

'Why did the police let you go?'

'Basically there's not enough evidence. Just because I was here on Christmas Eve doesn't mean I killed my aunt. I was in Athens on business before Christmas and popped over on the twenty-fourth to see Jennifer before flying back to London. My fingerprints aren't on the bottle of dessert wine and obviously they can't find any strychnine in my belongings. They asked the police in England to search my house in London this morning, but they didn't find any there either. Also, there was no arsenic in my belongings here or in my hotel room. They have no case whatsoever.'

'You could of course have been very clever. You are an intelligent man.'

'I am and I could have been, but I didn't do it. However, I want to know who did. It's completely beyond me. We have no other family as far as I know.'

'Perhaps you have and you aren't aware of it. Or perhaps Jennifer had an affair with a married man and she said she was going to tell his wife and he decided to get rid of her.'

'Ha! The prudish Jennifer . . . an affair!'

'Shows how well you knew her. She was all over my David. Luckily I'm secure enough in my relationship to not get worried.'

'And attractive enough.'

Eve blushed. She never tired of compliments, even from a potential killer.

'I've been on to her lawyers in England and here about her wills, but I don't think we'll know anything until the New Year,' James said.

'Damn. That might have told us if there was a secret member of the family. Were you expecting to get it all?'

'Not really. I reckon she's left it all to a cat's home or something like that. Anything but leave it to me. I have enough money so I'm not particularly bothered.'

'Oh, you can never have enough money,' Eve commented.

'James,' David exclaimed, coming into the room. 'You're out of jail.'

'Yes. The police didn't have enough evidence,' he said, deciding to leave it to Eve to elaborate. He knew he wasn't David's favourite person and now he'd finished his whisky he thought he'd get on his way. He desperately wanted to see Jane. James hoped she had faith in him and didn't think he was guilty. 'Well, thanks for listening to me, Eve, and not shutting the door in my face. I'm certain there are a lot of people who would.'

'Yes, Betty for one.'

'You don't know that, Eve,' David put in. 'She was quite taken by James.'

Eve grunted. David seemed to be criticising her a lot these days. Was he going off her? However, for once she decided to ignore him. 'I'll see you out, James. By the way, are you coming to

Annie and Pete's New Year's Eve party tomorrow?'

'I don't know if I'll be welcome.'

'I'll have a word with them. They're lovely people so I'm sure they won't mind. Unless you don't want to face people yet.'

'On the contrary. I have nothing to be ashamed of. I'm completely innocent so I'm not going to hide from anybody.'

Eve showed James out and as she shut the door, David came up to her. 'He's asked you to help him find the real killer, hasn't he?' David asked crossly. 'That is, if he isn't the murderer himself. I still have a feeling he is. Eve, I don't know how much more I can take. All this worrying about you, not knowing from one day to the next whether you're going to be alive or dead. I don't know if I can take it anymore. I'm sorry.' His voice was trembling as he spoke.

'David,' Eve said, starting to feel scared, 'he didn't ask anything of the sort. He only came to tell me he'd been released because there wasn't enough evidence to hold him. He didn't ask me to help him find the real killer, I promise.'

'But you're thinking about it, I know you are,' David replied, his voice rising.

'If it comes between you and looking for the killer, I choose you, David. I always would, believe me.'

'That's what you say now, but I know you. I'm even finding it hard to write now.'

'David, please — I promise I won't do anything.' She was really anxious now. Was David breaking up with her?

'I think I need to go home for a few days and think about things, Eve.' He turned away from her, head in hands.

'What things? Are we splitting up?' She put her hands on his shoulders, but he moved away. She couldn't believe this was happening. Had she really driven him out of her life?

'I don't know if we are breaking up, Eve. I have to think. I need time on my own.'

Eve was almost in tears, but she desperately tried to hold them back. She wasn't going to let him see her cry. She refused to be weak, even though that side of her might have been what would have kept David there. 'What about the party tomorrow?' she asked.

'I'm going to give it a miss. Perhaps you should too.'

'What will Betty think?' Eve wailed.

'Is that all you can think about, Eve? Betty? Our future's at stake and all you're worrying about is what Betty thinks. If that's all you're concerned about, then I don't think we have a future,' David said, getting angry now.

'Of course that's not all I care about. I love you, David.'

'And I love you, Eve, but you're a difficult woman to live with and I need time on my own. I'm going to pack my stuff and we'll speak in a few days' time.'

David turned and went up the stairs to get his things. He was trembling. He didn't want to leave her, but he had to be alone for a while. Eve kept getting into trouble and putting her life in danger. She had to pull herself together and grow up, otherwise there was no hope for them.

Eve felt tears falling down her cheeks. David couldn't see her like this so she called her dog, Portia, and they went out for a long walk in the countryside. She didn't care if she was well enough to walk far or not. She couldn't bear to see David go.

* * *

James left Eve's house feeling reasonably pleased. It had been a successful visit. Eve was willing to give him the benefit of the doubt as far as his innocence was concerned and she had come up with some pretty good ideas. She had been quite convinced by the idea that there was another member of the family around that he didn't know about. She was probably wondering now if it was someone in the ex-pat community here, or if it was a stranger who had come over on Christmas Eve from England with the sole purpose of killing his aunt. If only they knew what was in the will. Perhaps that would reveal more information. Unfortunately, everything looked like it could take a long time, and without their passports that meant he was stuck here on Crete, but so was Jane. *Thinking of it that way, things aren't all bad then!* He smiled.

As James got closer to the Phillips' house, he saw two people sitting outside. Who was that with Jane?

It's that prat, Paul. No sooner am I locked away than he makes a move on my girlfriend.

James was annoyed, but he decided his best course of action was to try and hide it. He was going to be a gentleman. After all, he wasn't going to stoop to Paul's level.

As he approached the house, Jane saw him. She jumped up and rushed to the gate. Paul sighed.

How on earth has he got out of jail? I was certain he was going to be put away for his aunt's murder.

'James,' Jane called out, smiling, 'you've been released.'

For the past half an hour Paul had been telling her all about Crete and had suggested they have a day out in Heraklion. She had almost been persuaded. He had been very sweet, telling her of a couple of monasteries they'd stop off at on the way. He was going to take her to a lovely taverna he knew in Heraklion for a bite to eat and a couple of glasses of wine. It sounded like a nice break from the village and the awful shock of James being arrested. However James was now back, as large as life, and Paul's offer was now completely forgotten.

'Yes, I'm free, Jane,' James replied as they walked towards Paul. 'The police didn't have enough evidence to hold me, but I swear to you, I didn't kill my aunt. Of course I can't have my passport back yet, like everyone else.'

'I'm so happy to see you. I knew you didn't do it. Come and have a drink.'

By this time Paul was fuming, but he decided to stay put. He wasn't going to leave Jane and James alone. 'Have they any other suspects?' he asked while Jane went to get James a drink.

'I have no idea. I think I'm the last person they would tell.'

'They're probably back to square one,' Jane said, sitting down.

'My aunt was a secretive woman. Goodness knows who she upset. It could be any number of people, I'm sure.'

'She hadn't been here for long though,' Paul remarked. 'Could she have aggravated somebody so much that that person would have wanted to kill her?'

'Looks like it,' Jane said. She was starting to get annoyed. Was Paul ever going to leave? She knew he was only staying to infuriate James, but James was being the perfect gentleman and wasn't even being rude to Paul.

However, she could see Paul was getting angry and the last thing she wanted was a fight to start. After all, Paul had no rights over her at all. James was her boyfriend, not Paul.

'I've been to see Eve,' James said a moment later.

'Oh,' Jane replied, looking anxious. 'Is everything all right with you two?'

'Yes, fine. We had a good chat. There are no hard feelings between the two of us.'

'Really?' Paul remarked. 'I don't think I'd ever speak to that woman again if she turned me in to the cops.'

'Ah well, that's where we differ.'

What does he mean by that? He's trying to make me look like the bad guy, thought Paul.

However, before Paul could say anything, they all saw Eve walking by with her dog. She had managed to stop crying now and had calmed down a little. She had decided that David wouldn't be able to live without her and would be back soon. She saw Paul sitting with Jane and James. She waved and Jane came running up to see her.

'Hello, Eve. Any ideas of how to get rid of Paul?' she whispered.

Eve wasn't in the mood for this. She still wanted to be on her own, but Jane looked so plaintive and in need of help. In addition, Eve felt guilty. She knew she had interfered badly in Jane's relationship with James, but it seemed as if Jane had forgiven her, so perhaps she had better make amends by helping her.

'I take it things are going well with James then?' Eve asked.

'Well, they could be if Paul would only leave. I'm sure he's only staying to be awkward. I'm certain James isn't the killer, Eve.'

'I don't think so either. I'm sorry he was arrested. I wouldn't have said anything to the police if I hadn't been poisoned. I was very scared that somebody had tried to kill me again. I have already spoken to James and we're back on good terms.'

She spoke hurriedly. She wanted to be friends again with Jane, especially after such an awful day. She might need a shoulder to cry on, and while she liked Annie, she might let it slip about the problems she was having with David, and then the whole village would know. Eve had totally forgotten about her guests, Alison and Robert. They had been going off on their own exploring the island, but she knew she would have to tell them what had happened between her and David. What would they say at Annie and Pete's party tomorrow? Robert was useless at keeping secrets. She had to stop thinking about all this. Jane needed help at the moment and it was better she kept her mind off David for the time being. Anyway, he'd probably come to his senses and realise how dull his life was without her.

'Right,' Eve said to Jane, 'I'll have a word with Paul.'

Jane breathed a sigh of relief. It was much better to have Eve as a friend than not. She always knew what to do in a crisis.

'Paul, just the man I wanted to see. I have a couple of plants which are dying before my very eyes. Do you think you could come over and have a quick look at them? If I leave it much longer, I think they will be well and truly gone.'

'What?' he replied, sounding slightly annoyed. 'Now?'

'If you could be a darling. I don't want to lose them. They were so pretty. I'm not that good at gardening, I'm afraid. Perhaps you'd come over once or twice a week to look after my garden, too? I'll pay you well.'

Eve was not short of a bob or two and Paul knew that. This was an offer he couldn't refuse. While work had started off well for him, recently people had been cutting down the number of hours they employed him, mainly due to the austerity measures in Greece and the extra taxes imposed. He couldn't turn down another job.

'Very well, I'll come and have a look.

Thank you for the beers, Jane. Will I see you at my brother and sister-in-law's party tonight?' He wanted to ask her to come with him, but with James there, he daren't. He knew James would butt in and say she was going as his date and she would agree. He was fed up of making a fool of himself. There must be some way of proving James was the murderer. After all, it was obviously him. Who else could it be?

'I haven't decided if I'm going yet,' Jane said to Paul. 'Perhaps.' She didn't want to go unless James went, but would he go? There would be so many staring faces there.

* * *

'Thank you for coming with me so promptly, Paul,' Eve said graciously.

'I know it was a ruse to get me to leave Jane and James alone,' Paul replied.

'Nonsense,' Eve said. 'I really do have dying flowers.

'That's as may be, but you still wanted to get me away from them. I'm not stupid, you know, but perhaps you are. James could still be the killer, and you've left Jane with a crazed madman.'

'I don't think James is a crazed madman, Paul. I don't even think he's the killer. But if he is, it was a cold calculated murder and it was his aunt he wanted to kill. I hardly see any reason for him to kill Jane.'

'I hope I don't have to remind you of that one day.'

Eve looked at Paul and felt a little sorry for him. He was very taken with Jane, but there was no future for him there, not even if James wasn't in the picture.

When they reached Eve's house, Paul went to look at the plants while Eve went to get them drinks. She didn't want to be alone in her house. Perhaps she should go and talk to Annie after all, but would she let it slip to Betty that she and David were taking a break from each other?

After Paul had given her instructions as to what to do with her plants, they sat down to have their drinks and then Alison and Robert arrived and joined them. 'Where's David?' Alison asked.

Eve didn't want to announce anything in front of Paul, so she lied. 'He's gone home to get some serious writing done. I'm afraid I've been rather a distraction this Christmas season.'

'Yes, you have,' Robert laughed. 'Ending up in hospital again. Poor old David.'

'What about poor old me?' Eve asked crossly. 'I was the one who nearly died.'

'Nearly died, my foot,' Robert continued. 'I bet that whoever did it could have killed you if they really wanted to. Both Alison and I think it was just a warning.'

Eve grunted. She preferred to think that somebody had tried to kill her. It sounded much more dramatic.

'Well I hope this has made you stop hunting for Jennifer's killer. It really is silly, not to mention dangerous. I bet next time it won't only be a warning,' Alison said.

'Yes,' Eve said. 'I finally agree with everybody. I am getting scared, plus there seem to be so few clues this time. I think I'll leave it to the experts.'

'Glad to hear it, Eve,' Robert put in. 'Never thought I'd hear the day though!'

'Right, I'd better be off now.' Paul got up, finishing his drink quickly. He wanted to get home. He felt humiliated after another rejection from Jane. This was the last time he would pursue her. It was pointless. 'I'll see you tonight?' he asked before he left.

'Tonight?' Eve asked. 'What's happening tonight?'

'Have you forgotten? I only mentioned it half an hour ago! My brother's having a do at his house. Don't say you won't be able to come. It's their first party since they moved here. They're a bit nervous nobody will turn up.'

'We'll be there,' Alison said. 'I don't know if Eve's up to it.'

Eve didn't feel like going, but she did feel sorry for Paul. He seemed to be having a lot of bad luck at the moment. 'I'll try,' she said, smiling weakly.

However, when Paul had gone, Eve burst into tears.

'What's wrong, Eve?' Alison said, rushing to put her arms around Eve. It wasn't often that the strong and secure Eve cried. It had to be something serious. Robert sat there, slightly embarrassed. He never knew what to do when women cried, especially not someone as tough as Eve.

'I can't go to Lucy and Kevin's party tonight,' wailed Eve. 'I'll be alone. David and I have had a big argument. He's gone home. He hates me. He probably won't want to speak to me again.'

'There, there, Eve,' Alison said, trying to comfort her friend. 'I'm sure that whatever he said was in the heat of the moment and when he calms down, he'll be back.'

'No, he won't. This was a big row.

It'll take a lot for him to get over it. I'm too scared to go over and see him.'

Although Eve had decided only a little while ago that David would be back because he wouldn't be able to live without her, now she had changed her mind again. Now it was all over.

'Well, I'd leave him be,' Robert put in. 'I bet I know what it was all about, Eve. It was about you and all your attempts at detective work, wasn't it?'

Eve looked at him sheepishly.

'I knew it,' Robert said. 'I'm not surprised one bit. I mean, you ended up in hospital again. David's in love with you and he doesn't want to go through all the pain of losing you.'

'I've hardly done anything this time,' Eve said, wiping away her tears with a hanky.

'Well you did enough to get poisoned, didn't you? And I bet if you got another clue you'd be off searching for the killer again, wouldn't you?' Robert asked.

Eve refused to answer.

'Well,' he continued, 'you can't stay in tonight just because you've argued with David.'

'What will Betty say?'

'Oh for goodness sake, forget about Betty. She's so unimportant. Just say David's busy working.'

'What if David turns up?'

'Stop making excuses, Eve,' Robert said crossly. 'I'll check with him for you if you like, but I doubt if he'll be there. Now go and have a bath and start getting ready.'

Once Eve had gone upstairs, Alison went and put her arms around Robert. 'My, my, Robert, I do like it when you're forceful.'

'Thank you, darling. It's one of my hidden attributes!'

She smiled at him as he bent down and kissed her. He was looking forward to coming back from the party that evening.

11

That evening Eve was the first person downstairs for a change. She sat waiting nervously for Alison and Robert, wishing that she wasn't going out. She hadn't taken quite as long with her hair and make-up, not feeling in any mood for getting dressed up and partying, but she had still made an effort and looked as attractive as usual. She didn't want anyone to know there was anything wrong.

When Alison and Robert came downstairs, they were surprised to see Eve waiting for them. It was most unusual. Robert was concerned to see there was a drink in her hand. 'I hope you haven't had too many of those,' he said, looking anxious.

'Only one,' she replied harshly. 'And it wasn't even a large measure of gin. Just needed a little Dutch courage, that's all.' *It's none of their business*, she thought. *It's me that's got to get through this evening, not them*.

However, she was wrong. Both Robert and Alison were dreading the night ahead, not knowing how Eve was going to act. They didn't think she looked at all tipsy, but Eve had always been able to keep control, however much she had drunk. But these were exceptional circumstances, and who knew what she might spring on them? Alison was worried about other things as well. Eve didn't want Betty to know about her and David falling out with each other, but Robert could often let things slip. On top of everything, Eve was her own worst enemy. It was highly likely that she would act strangely and make people wonder where David was.

Earlier in the evening, after Eve had gone to have a bath, Robert had quickly popped over to David's house. As soon as David opened the door, Robert realised how upset he was about the whole situation. David had told him he still loved Eve, but he didn't know if he could cope with her putting her life in danger all the time. Robert had told him how miserable Eve was as well, but David had still said he needed a few days on his own. He had also said he wasn't going to the party that evening and he wouldn't tell anybody that they had split up, especially not Betty.

'I was angry with Eve because she was so bothered about Betty knowing we were having a break from each other, but I wouldn't hurt her by going to the party alone. I'm not a cruel and heartless man, Robert, and anyway, I'm gradually going off Betty. She's tried to interfere in our relationship too much. I certainly don't want her gloating and upsetting Eve. I hope you and Alison will keep this to yourself.'

'Of course we will. I know I sometimes let things slip, but I'll be more than careful with this news, I promise.'

'Thanks, Robert. It's appreciated.'

Eve was relieved to hear that David wasn't going to Kevin and Lucy's that evening, and she had even prepared her story. David was on a deadline to finish his book and was way behind. However, she was worried about the following evening. How was she going to make an excuse for David not going to the New Year's Eve party at Annie and Pete's? Nobody would believe he would be working on his novel on New Year's Eve. There was nothing for it. She couldn't go. She would have to pretend to be ill.

* * *

Meanwhile, Jane was getting ready to be picked up by James and was feeling excited that he was accompanying her again. Just think, this time yesterday evening her world had collapsed. James had been arrested for the murder of his aunt, but now he had been released and they were going to a party together. What was even better, they were going alone and were not being escorted by Eve and David.

Jane was looking forward to walking into the party with James. She expected that Paul would already be there, as it was his brother's party. This should convince him that she wasn't interested in him at all. Why did he have to persist in chasing her? She felt sorry for him, but she was getting fed up with his perseverance.

Jane glanced at herself in the mirror. She knew she looked attractive, but she did have to get some new clothes. None of hers were as seductive as Eve's midnight-blue dress which she had lent her. However she couldn't wear that again. She should have thought earlier in the day and asked to borrow something else, but she had totally forgotten. She'd have to remember to ask her tonight if she could borrow a dress for the New Year's Eve party.

Jane heard a knock at the door and her stomach did a somersault. It must be James. She went to answer the door and was pleased that she had been right. James stood there, tall, handsome and sophisticated, looking very smart in a suit and tie. She knew he would show up everybody else. The other men didn't know how to dress to go out in the evening, especially not Paul. He looked scruffy in jeans and T-shirts most of the time. It didn't take much to make an effort, did it?

'Good evening, Jane,' James said. 'You look beautiful this evening, as always. These are for you.' He handed her a bouquet of red roses. She was impressed.

'James, they're wonderful. Thank you. Come in. I'll just put them in water.'

When she came back, she asked him if he wanted a drink, but he said they'd better go. Unlike Eve, he didn't like to be too late at any social gathering. 'I'm looking forward to spending this evening with you, Jane,' he said.

'Me too,' she replied. 'I only hope that people are civil to you.'

'I'm sure most people will be, but there will be the odd one or two who will still be convinced I'm the killer. Come on, let's go and get our entrance over and done with.'

'Okay. At least you know that Eve and I are on your side.'

'Yes, and I'm sure Eve will have something to say if anyone starts criticising me.'

'Oh, I have no doubt about that, James, no doubt at all!'

* * *

For a change, Eve left home reasonably early to go to a party, not much caring what anyone thought. Did it matter anymore if she was fashionably late? Did anything matter?

As they walked there, Eve kept reminding Alison and Robert that they couldn't tell anyone about her and David.

'Of course we're not going to tell anyone, Eve,' Robert finally said, a little irately. 'We're your friends, as you should well know, and we're here to give you support, not to make things worse.'

'I know you are,' Eve replied, almost feeling guilty. 'But sometimes it is easy to let things slip without thinking.'

At least she was subtle enough not to say that Robert often told secrets, albeit by accident.

'We won't tell anyone, we promise,' Alison said, putting an arm around Eve.

'Thank you,' Eve said graciously, hoping they would keep their mouths shut.

As soon as they arrived at Kevin and Lucy's, Betty spotted them, and seeing no sign of David, went straight up to Eve.

'No David then?' Betty asked her immediately.

'Not this evening, Betty. He has a deadline to meet with his agent and he's getting behind, so he's gone home to concentrate on his writing. We've done too much socialising over the Christmas period, I'm afraid.'

'What a pity. I was looking forward to seeing him this evening. Well, there's always tomorrow, isn't there?'

Eve smiled and nodded, but she was concerned about New Year's Eve. Betty had been very quick to come up and ask about David, and Eve was pretty sure she was already thinking there was something fishy going on.

Annie came up shortly afterwards and kissed Eve on the cheek. Eve had to go through the same questioning, and even though Annie was a good friend, Eve didn't tell her the truth. She was certain Annie would let it slip and then everybody would know. Eve suddenly wished she were back in London. News never travelled so fast there.

Kevin and Lucy came up to greet Eve, pleased to see that she had been well enough to come to their party, but then James and Jane made an entrance and the room went quiet. A couple of people didn't even know that James had been released.

'James, how did you get out of jail?' a loud voice boomed. 'Hope you didn't break out!'

'No, Betty,' he replied. 'I was released. There wasn't enough evidence to hold me.'

'Well I knew all along it wasn't you,' she replied. 'A gentleman like you would never commit a murder.'

Stupid woman. What would she know? Paul thought, jealously watching James and Jane together.

'Well, you're welcome in our home,' Lucy said. 'Come and get drinks, both of you.'

That's strange, thought Eve. *The other day she told me she didn't like the man. Well, I suppose she can't throw him out, especially as he's been released by the police.*

Paul, however, was having other thoughts. *Everybody's pandering to him. Why? What on earth has that man got? He thinks he's better than everyone else, but he isn't. I'll show him. Just wait and see.*

Paul was getting angrier by the second and Eve was watching him and could see it. She was concerned. He certainly had a temper and she could almost imagine him murdering someone, but she couldn't think why he would want to kill Jennifer. She needed to find out more about him to see if he had a motive.

Eve got herself a gin and tonic, thinking it was safer to get her own drinks, and went over to chat to Don, but she was missing David. She had got used to him being around and she would have loved to talk to him about Paul and how she suspected him of killing Jennifer. However, this was what had got her into trouble. She couldn't discuss this case with David, or in fact any other case. She shouldn't even be thinking about who murdered Jennifer.

As the evening wore on, Eve got bored. It wasn't the same without David, but she had spent years doing things on her own and had never minded, so why couldn't she get back to how things had been? She was a self-sufficient and secure woman who hadn't needed anyone to enjoy life, but she now realised that her life had changed. She liked to do things with David and she missed him when he wasn't there. She had finally met someone she wanted to spend her life with, but she had probably blown it.

She knew she should put the murder out of her mind if she wanted any chance of getting David back, but it was difficult. It was far too interesting and she needed this stimulation. Why couldn't she have both David and the excitement of the murder?

A little later on Eve came out of the upstairs bathroom, having retouched her make-up, ready to say her good-byes. She wanted to look good when she had the attention of everyone. Passing one of the bedrooms, she heard raised voices and as usual, curiosity got the better of her. She slowly crept towards the door, which was slightly ajar, and tried her best to listen. Within a few seconds, she realised it was Kevin and Lucy arguing.

Really, she thought, *can't they wait till we've gone? They have guests to look after*.

'Do you have to keep looking at Eve, Kev? It's pretty obvious to everyone that you fancy her,' Lucy hissed.

Eve gasped. She hadn't even been

aware of this. So many men were attracted to her, and she had come to barely notice them unless she was particularly interested or they made a nuisance of themselves. As for Kevin, he was hardly appealing, plus he was married.

'Oh shut up, you stupid woman. You're imagining things.'

'What? Like I imagined that one-night stand you had with Jennifer Anderson?'

Eve gasped again. She had to get back downstairs before they saw her. Lucy could be the killer and she could have poisoned her as well. There was no way she was going to let that woman see her.

'I thought we'd got over that, Lucy. You've got to forget it — and most of all, stop mentioning it. What if someone hears you? They could think you're the killer and tell the police. God knows you've got a motive.'

'What? Do you really think I killed that obnoxious woman, Kevin? Do you think I'm capable of murder?'

'I honestly don't know, Lucy.'

'How can you say that?' she replied, now almost in tears. 'Haven't you hurt me enough?'

'Oh, for God's sake. Don't pretend to be in love with me. That ship sailed a long time ago.'

Lucy stared at him. There was no point pretending. She had stopped loving Kevin many years ago when he'd had his first affair.

'Underneath that quiet shell there's an obnoxious, angry woman. Nobody but me sees you when you get like this. If they did, they'd be shocked.'

Eve still stood by the door listening. She knew she should leave, but this was far too interesting.

'That's different to murder. I could never take another person's life, never,' Lucy wailed. She was now in tears.

'I don't know if I believe that or not, but we can't stay here all night. We have guests downstairs. I had better go and see to them.'

Eve didn't know what to do. If she went down the stairs, Kevin might see her and wonder if she had heard anything. She thought she'd better go back in the loo.

Eve stayed in the bathroom for over five minutes before deciding it was safe to come out. However, as she walked past Kevin and Lucy's bedroom, Lucy appeared. Eve stopped, knowing she had to act normally. Lucy couldn't know that she had overheard her conversation with her husband.

'Lovely party, Lucy,' Eve said, smiling, even though she felt herself trembling.

'Thank you, Eve. It's a pity David couldn't come.'

'Yes it is, but he is very dedicated to his work, I'm afraid,' Eve replied, moving towards the stairs. She didn't want to prolong the conversation any longer than necessary. Kevin thought his wife was capable of murder, so she could be in real danger and she wanted to get downstairs as soon as possible. 'I should get going soon however,' she said. 'I want to see how David's getting on.'

'Oh, not before I bring out the cakes and desserts, Eve. You don't want to miss those.'

'Okay,' Eve replied. She decided, however, that she didn't want Lucy to give her any food or drinks, not wanting to risk being poisoned again. It was quite possible that Lucy had killed Jennifer and poisoned her.

When Eve came downstairs she saw Alison and Robert holding on to each other in a slow dance. James and Jane were doing the same and Eve suddenly felt sad and lonely. She missed David terribly. However, this feeling didn't last long as Paul marched over to her.

'I hope you're satisfied with your meddling,' he spat at her.

'What?' she asked, shocked to hear him speak in such a manner.

'I'm sure James is the killer, and he's all over Jane. If he murders her, it'll all be your fault.'

'I doubt if he is the killer,' Eve replied calmly. 'There are many more likely suspects.'

'Yeah, who?'

'I think you'd be the last person I'd tell, Paul. The last person.'

Paul's eyes filled with anger and he grabbed Eve by the throat and tried to strangle her in full view of everyone. Pete and James were the first to see what was happening and dashed to her rescue. The two men managed to pull Paul off Eve in no time at all and Annie and Jane went over to comfort her. Eve was bent over coughing, unable to believe what Paul had tried to do.

Why on earth did he do that? Eve thought. *Perhaps he's the killer. Perhaps he had a night of passion with Jennifer, and she rejected him afterwards*.

'What on earth is wrong with you, Paul?' Pete asked.

'Nothing,' he replied. He couldn't think of what to say. What had come over him? He had suddenly become so angry watching James and Jane dancing in each others' arms, and then he saw Eve and he flipped. However, he didn't want to admit to everyone how much he liked Jane and that he still thought James was the killer. What good would it do? It wouldn't win Jane back, would it?

'What on earth has Eve done to make you attack her like that?' James asked.

'It's between me and her,' he said.

'The hell it is,' Eve said, recovering from her ordeal. She was well and truly fed up with Paul and now everybody would know what an idiot he was. 'Basically he still thinks James is Jennifer's killer. To top it all, he fancies Jane. Because I helped to get Jane together with James originally, Paul says it'll be my fault if James kills Jane. There you have it. Ridiculous.'

'Oh Paul,' Jane said first, 'how could you think of such things? James would never kill me. And as for attacking Eve, that was a terrible thing to do. She's my friend. I'm afraid I wouldn't go out with you even if James wasn't here.

You're not my type. I'm sorry.'

Paul hung his head in shame. This party was turning into a disaster and he had made a fool of himself. Eve was going to pay for this.

'Yes,' James joined in. 'You have a warped mind, Paul. I should be angry with you, but I'm not. Instead I feel sorry for you. You need help.'

'I don't need your help or anyone else's, thank you.' With that, he stormed out without telling his brother or sister-in-law where he was going.

Everybody was silent until Kevin spoke. 'I expect we all feel a bit subdued and you want to go home, but please stay for Lucy's desserts. She spent a long time preparing them.'

Most people nodded and started to dig in as soon as they arrived.

'How are you holding up?' Annie asked Eve.

'I'm okay I think,' Eve replied. 'He's got a bit of a temper, hasn't he?'

'Yes he has. I bet you wish David was here.'

'Not really. He'd probably say I've been meddling again when I haven't, I really haven't.'

Alison came up and handed a plate of desserts and cakes to Eve. 'I didn't think you'd want to get up, so I got you a bit of everything.'

'Oh, how lovely. Thank you, Alison.'

As she ate, forgetting completely that she was going to get her own deserts, Eve started thinking. Now there were two suspects in the case, Lucy and Paul; perhaps even three. Kevin could also have killed Jennifer. Perhaps he had wanted a one-night stand while she'd wanted more. He could have killed her to get her out of the way. However, this was less likely because Lucy knew, so Jennifer couldn't have threatened to go and tell his wife. No, Eve decided Lucy and Paul were the most likely suspects, but it was going to be difficult to prove. She wished David were here to help her, but he had gone and she had no idea if he'd ever return.

12

Eve woke up late the next day. It was after ten and she jumped out of bed, not knowing how it had been possible for her to sleep so soundly. She thought she would have had nightmares after that awful party the night before. Paul had been so angry he had wanted to kill her . . . And then there was the argument between Kevin and Lucy. She was certain Lucy knew she had been listening, and if Lucy were the killer she would surely try to silence her next. This was unbelievable. She hadn't even been searching for the murderer, yet all these suspects kept appearing. How did David expect her to keep away from the murder? It just wouldn't leave her alone.

She got out of bed and looked in the mirror. She wasn't happy with what she saw. Her eyes were puffy and her neck was red where Paul had grabbed her. She still couldn't believe his strength. He had seemed such a sad, lonely fellow. *Just goes to show*, she mused.

She decided to wash her hair and do her make-up even before she went downstairs to have a coffee. Normally she wouldn't bother, but she had guests and didn't want them to see her looking like this.

Forty-five minutes later Eve came down the stairs looking more like her old self, but when she saw David sitting on her sofa she burst into tears, ruining all her efforts. He jumped up and rushed over, taking her in his arms.

'Eve, stop that. I'm back now. Robert came over this morning and told me what happened at the party last night. I know you didn't do anything to provoke such a reaction from Paul. I've half a mind to go over and have it out with him, but Robert thinks it's best left alone.'

'Yes, David, it probably is,' she said, pulling away slightly so she could look at him. 'He's a little crazy, I think, but that's not all. Oh dear . . . ' She started sobbing again.

'What is it?' David asked, his heart pounding.

'I wasn't doing anything planned, I promise, but I overheard something last night which could tell us who murdered Jennifer. I don't know if either of the people talking knows I overheard them, but unfortunately it's possible.'

'Oh, Eve,' David sighed.

'I promise you, it wasn't deliberate. I went upstairs to use the bathroom, and as I came out I heard Kevin and Lucy arguing in the bedroom. Apparently Kevin had a one-night stand with Jennifer and Lucy can't seem to get over it. It's a perfect reason for murder, don't you think?'

Alison gasped. 'Yes it is,' she said. 'Wow, to think it might be Lucy. She seems so dull and quiet.'

'I don't think she really is,' Eve replied. 'Kevin talked about her vile temper and how we'd all be surprised if we saw that side of her.'

'I only hope they don't suspect you overheard them,' David put in.

'I was about to go down the stairs when I heard Kevin about to leave the bedroom. So I went back in the bathroom. Unfortunately, when I came back out Lucy was there, so I think she may suspect that I heard them arguing.'

'Damn,' Robert said. 'Perhaps you should go to the police with this information. If she is the killer, she'll probably go after you.'

'I don't know. It's not very concrete evidence, and if she finds out it came from me that'll give her an excuse to get rid of me.'

'She wouldn't dare,' Alison said. 'Not if the police are watching her.'

'I don't know,' Eve said. 'I really don't know what to do.'

'I think you should tell the police, Eve,' David said, 'rather than trying to find out more on your own.'

Eve knew he would say that. He didn't want her to try and find the murderer herself, knowing that she could be risking her life again. However, the case was getting interesting and she didn't want to tell the police what she knew quite yet. She would much rather hand the murderer over to the police herself, but David had come back and she didn't want him to leave again. She felt much safer with him around.

'Do you really think Lucy is a murderer?' Eve continued. 'I would have thought Kevin was also a possibility. Perhaps he was fed up with Jennifer pestering him so he decided that getting rid of her was the only answer.'

'You could be right,' David replied. 'But either way it's highly likely one of them is dangerous, and you need to keep your distance.'

'If they're determined to kill me they will, David, mark my words,' Eve said. 'There'll be nothing I can do.'

'Well, you'd better keep your mouth shut from now on, and one of us needs to be with you all the time.' The others nodded in agreement.

'Yes,' Robert said. 'However much you hate it, we're going to be sticking to you like glue.'

'Great,' Eve sighed. 'Just great.'

'Come on, Eve,' David said. 'You had an exhausting day yesterday and a traumatic evening. You probably still need some rest. You look like you haven't had much sleep, and I'm sure that by the afternoon your mind will be clearer and you'll know what's the best thing to do.'

'Surprisingly I did sleep and didn't have any nightmares, but perhaps I will lie down for a bit. I still feel a little shaky after last night.'

'Well, you need to be wide awake for the New Year's Eve party tonight,' David said, smiling.

'You mean you're coming?' Eve asked happily. David nodded and Eve suddenly felt hopeful after all the gloom and doom she had been experiencing.

'Sleep well, Eve,' Alison said as Eve went up the stairs.

However, this was the last thing she did. She was more than relieved that David had returned home and she wouldn't have to go to the New Year's Eve party alone. However, this wasn't the only reason. She really did love him and could hardly believe he was back, but despite what had happened at the party, her juices were flowing. She wasn't prepared to hand over what she knew to the police. She wanted to find out more herself, but how was she to do this without alienating David again?

Eve finally got up again around one and when she went downstairs, David was working on his novel. 'Hello darling,' he said. 'Did you get much sleep?'

'Finally,' Eve said, smiling. 'Where are Alison and Robert?'

'They've gone out for some lunch and a drive. They thought we'd want some time alone.'

'Oh,' Eve whispered, wondering what this was going to be about. *Is he going to make me promise not to search for*

Jennifer's murderer? I can't do it. I've got to find some way of making it sound like I am promising to give it up when I'm not really.

'Come and sit on the sofa, Eve,' David said. She went over meekly. 'I know the murder excites you, but it worries me sick thinking about losing you, darling.'

'I know,' Eve replied. 'But I don't know much this time. To tell you the truth, I think the police would laugh at me if I went to them with the information I have about Lucy and Kevin. I'll not bother.'

'I don't know about that, Eve. It is a possibility.'

'Oh, I doubt it. I'll wait until after the New Year anyway.'

'All right, but I still think you should tell them.' David paused for a moment.

'They'll think I've been snooping again.'

'Better than being attacked by Lucy. That is, if she is the killer.'

Eve gave David a hug, a tear falling.

'Hey, what's up?'

'Oh, I'm just remembering Paul trying to strangle me last night. I know he wouldn't have managed it with everybody else being there, but it was still pretty frightening.'

'It must have been. I'm sorry I let you go on your own,' David said, wiping away her tears. He lightly kissed her and she felt a sigh of relief, knowing she had him back.

'Right, I'm off to the local shop to get a few things,' she said. 'I'll see you in a bit.'

'I should go with you, darling,' David replied.

'Don't be silly. You can't go everywhere with me. If I'm not back in fifteen minutes, send out the search parties.'

David smiled, but he was worried. He knew he couldn't follow Eve all the time, despite what he had said earlier. It would drive her crazy, but he knew he would be nervous every time she was out of his sight.

* * *

Eve didn't need to get much so she decided to walk to the shops. As she was strolling along, she heard a voice behind her.

'Eve, wait. Wait a moment.'

She turned and saw Jane running behind her.

'Jane, hi. How are you?'

'Oh, I'm fine, but how are you after that awful man attacked you at the party last night? I couldn't believe it. I never liked him much. Well, I did a bit in the beginning, but then I thought there was something slightly odd about him. And now . . . gosh, attacking you so horribly. It was awful. He could have killed you.'

'Well, if we had been on our own, he might have done.'

'What on earth was it all about?'

'I don't think you want to know.'

'Oh no, it wasn't about me, about my relationship with James?'

'Unfortunately he blames me for

getting you together with James. He thinks he would have been with you if it wasn't for me.'

'He's crazy. I wouldn't go out with him even if I wasn't seeing James. He's living in a dream world. I'm so sorry this happened because of me.'

'Don't be, Jane. He's a little mad. He couldn't stand seeing you dance with James and suddenly went potty. It's hardly your fault.'

'I hope he doesn't cause any problems at the New Year's Eve party tonight,' Jane mumbled.

'I hope he doesn't come.'

Both girls laughed. Then Eve spotted Dimitris Kastrinakis, the police officer, outside the shop and wondered if she should tell him about the Fowlers after all.

Why not? David's not going to give me a chance to solve this murder on my own this time. And if Lucy thinks I suspect her, it's better the police are keeping an eye on her.

'I've got to go and have a word with

the police officer, Jane. Will you excuse me?'

'Of course,' Jane replied. 'See you tonight.'

Eve walked up to Dimitris, finding she was trembling. She imagined he would think she had been meddling. Plus, she wondered if she would regret doing this. Was she giving up her chance of fame?

'Ah, Miss Masters. I hear that Mr Paul Fowler attacked you at a party last night.'

'My goodness,' she replied, 'news travels fast. Yes, he did. He is slightly crazy, I believe. He was upset because he saw James and Jane dancing and believes I had something to do with them getting together. What he can't get into his head is that even if I hadn't, Jane wouldn't have gone out with him. She can't stand him.'

'I'm pleased it was nothing to do with the murder.'

'Ah, that,' she murmured.

'Oh no,' Dimitris replied. 'What have

you done now?'

'I haven't done anything, but I overheard something that might be relevant. Instead of doing anything, I'm telling you. You see, I'm being sensible.'

Dimitris shook his head. He couldn't believe that she wasn't going to do something with this information, whatever it was. Perhaps she was going to see if she could prove who the killer was quicker than the police. That would be more like her.

'So what did you overhear, madam?'

'Well, last night when I was at Kevin and Lucy Fowlers' party, I went to the bathroom upstairs and when I walked by Kevin and Lucy's bedroom, I heard them talking and I stopped to listen. The gist of it was that Kevin had had a one-night stand with Jennifer Anderson and Lucy found out about it. Naturally she wasn't too happy; in fact she was very angry.'

'That is very interesting, especially as both of them had denied knowing her when we questioned them.' Dimitris was becoming curious about all of the Fowler family. Either Kevin or Lucy could have killed Jennifer, and Paul had a foul temper. He might also have had a connection with the deceased.

'So,' Eve asked, 'are you going to question them?'

'That is procedure.'

'Do you need anything else from me?

'Not at the moment, madam. Thank you for this information.'

Dimitris put out his hand to shake Eve's and then he went on his way. Eve hoped Kevin and Lucy wouldn't find out it was her who told the police about their conversation.

13

The New Year's Eve bash was being held at the Black Cat, but everybody had decided to make it more of a communal event, rather than Ken and Jan selling tickets. They would charge for drinks as usual, but all the people going had clubbed together to book a band for the evening and for the food. Annie and Jan had agreed to do most of the catering between them, with Betty making a couple of desserts. Eve had shocked Betty by saying that she was excusing herself from any of the cooking, telling her friends that she would be busy with her guests. In reality, she didn't want her dishes to be mixed with the other ones and somebody else getting credit for what she had cooked. She preferred to cater for a party on her own so that everybody knew that she had cooked everything herself. She had conveniently forgotten about the Christmas cake which she had bought from the English shop for her own get-together.

The party started at eight, but by half past, Eve still wasn't ready. Robert shouted up the stairs: 'Come on, Eve; I'm starving.'

'Yes, we all are,' added Alison.

David didn't bother to say anything, knowing this would only infuriate Eve. She would probably take even longer with her make-up and making a decision as to what to wear. He didn't know why she bothered to take so much time. Eve looked stunning in anything she put on.

At last Eve came down the stairs looking even more striking than David had expected. She was wearing a long black dress, which was unusual for her as she normally wore short dresses and skirts. However, this dress clung to her body, showing off her figure to best advantage. There wasn't an ounce of fat on Eve, and Alison sighed. Alison had a lovely hourglass figure, but she could put on a few pounds and she knew she had over Christmas.

Eve had put her blonde hair up for a change, and her new diamond earrings dangled. They were a Christmas present from David and he was pleased that she was wearing them this evening. He wanted to touch her soft, silky skin, which still had a hint of brown, but Alison and Robert were waiting to go.

'Are we going then? We don't want to be too late,' Eve said, as if she had been waiting for them.

'God, you're impossible,' Robert said grumpily.

Alison laughed. It was fun staying at Eve's, despite the poisonings, murders, break-ups and arguments.

* * *

In the Fowlers' house, Kevin and Lucy were getting ready for the New Year's Eve party. 'What a terrible day,' said Kevin. 'I'd rather stay at home tonight.

Do we have to go, Lucy?'

'Yes, we do. They'd all be wondering where we are, especially the person who turned us in.'

'Who could have done it?' Kevin asked his wife. 'Only Paul knows about my night with Jennifer, and he wouldn't have said anything to the police. I'm pretty sure of that. I'm just relieved they didn't throw us in jail. We've both got a motive to kill her.'

'There's no real evidence though, Kevin.' She continued to put on her make-up. She was fed up with looking plain while the likes of Eve and Jane went around all dolled up and pretty. *But who else knew about Kevin and Jennifer? I've got to find out. There's something at the back of my mind, but I can't think what it is, not for the life of me*.

'Come on, Lucy; what on earth are you putting all that muck on for?' Kevin asked impatiently.

'Oh shut up, Kevin, and leave me alone. I've every right to make myself look nice.'

'It'll take more than a bit of war-paint to do that,' he replied nastily.

'Carry on like that and I'll be going to the police and telling them that you crept out on Christmas Eve and I didn't know where you where going. They'll think it was you who killed Jennifer.'

'I doubt it, dear. They'll wonder why you didn't tell them earlier and think you've got something to hide.'

'We're not the only suspects, Kevin. I'm sure they think Paul might have done it after his performance last night. He really went for Eve.'

'Yes, he did,' Kevin said, smiling.

'I'm amazed to see you smile. I thought you were fond of your brother.'

'I am, but if it's between me and him going to jail, I'd rather it was him.'

'And then there's James,' Lucy put in. 'I'm sure the police haven't discounted him even though they've released him. I'm sure he's got a motive. After all, he was Jennifer's nephew.'

'It wouldn't surprise me; it wouldn't

surprise me at all. Look, let's get going to this party. And put on a good show, Lucy. I only hope nobody saw the police come into our house. You know how quickly gossip travels in these villages. They'll have us guilty in no time.'

'I know. I wish we weren't going.'

'That would make us look even guiltier, dear.'

* * *

Betty was putting on her earrings. 'So, do you think they suspect either Kevin or Lucy, Don?'

'For goodness sake, how many more times are you going to ask me that? I have absolutely no idea.'

An acquaintance of Betty's had seen the police going into the Fowlers' house earlier in the day and had been straight on the phone to Betty asking if she knew anything about it. Betty hated having to say she didn't. She usually knew everything that was going on.

'They must be suspects in Jennifer's

murder, don't you think, Don? Otherwise why would the police have visited them?'

'They might be, but you can't ask them outright this evening. It would be extremely rude.'

'Not half as rude as killing somebody.'

'Good grief, woman,' Don said, his voice rising. He was a mild-mannered man and usually shut his ears to Betty's rants and ravings, but now she was going too far.

'You are not — I repeat, not — going to say anything to either of them about this tonight. Do you hear me?'

Betty was silent. She had never heard Don speak to her so harshly before.

'I said, do you hear me?'

'Yes, Don. I won't say a word.' *My goodness*, she thought. *He's being so forceful. I could almost fall in love with him again*.

'Right, Betty, let's get going.'

'Yes, Don. I'll get my jacket.'

Don felt himself trembling. It had

been a long time since he'd spoken to Betty like this, but it did feel good. She went too far a lot of the time and upset so many people. It was about time he took control.

* * *

Eve and David walked into the Black Cat with Alison and Robert. She was relieved that she didn't have to come alone, especially after the previous evening and Paul's unexpected attack on her. In fact, she had almost decided she wouldn't attend if she had to come without her darling David.

Thinking about it, Paul's behaviour was very odd. They had been getting on well until she had set up Jane with James. But still, she would never have expected him to try and strangle her.

Eve's eyes then caught Betty's and she could tell that her arch-enemy was upset to see that David was with her. She knew Betty had hoped she had had an argument with David and had perhaps broken up with him. Eve was happy she had proved her wrong, but of course it could all have been so different. Eve shivered, thinking about what the alternative could have been.

She naturally put on a good show for Betty, and was very affectionate towards David. He didn't mind too much, despite not usually going in for public displays of affection. However, he allowed her to do what she wanted because of the difficult time she had experienced at the party the previous evening, plus today she had actually done as he wished and had given the police information about the murder. He could hardly believe it when she told him that she had met Dimitris Kastrinakis and had told him about Kevin and Lucy's argument.

However, Eve was slightly worried and kept looking around for the Fowlers, but they hadn't arrived yet. Had they been arrested? She didn't think there was enough evidence for an arrest, but perhaps she was wrong.

Jane and James spotted Eve and David and came up to them. 'Good evening,' James said. 'I'm pleased to see you here, Eve. No lasting effects after last night then?'

'No, I'm fine, thank you.'

'I'm here to protect her now,' David said. He still didn't much care for James.

'Perhaps Paul won't come tonight,' Alison said.

'No such luck,' Jane put in. 'He's just come in with his brother and Lucy.'

'Ignore him,' Robert said.

'I don't think she'll be able to,' James said. He's coming over. What do you want?' he asked Paul harshly. They all turned and David moved to protect Eve.

'Just a word with Eve, if you don't mind.'

'Well, she doesn't want to talk to you,' David said severely.

'It's all right, David. I'll talk to Paul for a moment.'

'Eve . . . '

'David, you're here. He's hardly going to try anything.'

David and I will be watching. And Robert,' James put in.

David grimaced. Why did James have to interfere? Eve was his woman and he was the one to protect her, not James.

Eve moved away with Paul.

'I want to apologise, Eve. I don't know what came over me last night.'

'I don't either, Paul. You were like a crazed person. I would never have imagined it of you.'

'Well, the police gave me a good talking-to.'

'I didn't call them, Paul.'

'Apparently James went in this morning and reported it. He said I had a violent temper and thought they should know. I think he's trying to pin the murder of Jennifer on me.'

'Why should he do that?'

'He despises me. It's probably because he knows I like Jane, but he knows I've got no chance with her, so why should he worry?'

'Perhaps he's insecure underneath it all.'

'I doubt it. He's got everything going

for him and Jane's obsessed with him.'

'I'm sorry, Paul.'

'Well, that's life. Anyway, I apologise again about yesterday.'

'Let's forget it. Okay?'

'Thanks, Eve.'

Eve went back to the others, thinking what a much nicer person she'd become in the past few months. Before, she'd never have forgiven him.

'So, what did he want, darling?' David asked.

'He apologised for last night.'

'You didn't forgive him?' James jumped in.

'Yes. There's no point holding grudges.'

James shook his head. Eve wasn't the bitch he'd heard she was. However, David was proud of her. Despite not liking Paul and not thinking he deserved forgiveness, Eve had been a better person than he would have been. She had come on leaps and bounds in the past few months. She wasn't this forgiving when she had landed in Crete in August.

The men went to get the drinks and

Eve turned her attention to Jane. 'Well, you look radiant this evening.'

'I'm so happy, Eve. James is a wonderful man. I can't believe how lucky I am.'

Eve and Alison looked at each other and smiled, but Eve saw Kevin and Lucy and she became anxious. What if they thought it was her who had gone to the police, and one of them was the killer? She could be their next victim.

'What's up?' Alison asked Eve when Jane went to the ladies'. 'You look as if you've seen a ghost.'

'Oh, nothing, really. Just wondering if anybody's going to try and kill me again, that's all.'

'Oh, Eve, why should they? You've been as good as gold.'

'What about Kevin or Lucy? It's highly likely one of them killed Jennifer, or perhaps they both decided to get rid of her. And if they find out I went to the police, they could get rid of me next.'

'The police would suspect them straight away, so I doubt if they will try anything. And anyway, the more I think about it, the less likely I think one of them killed Jennifer. They don't seem like murderers. If Lucy knew about the night Kevin spent with Jennifer, he would have had no need to silence her; and if Kevin had promised never to see Jennifer again, why would Lucy want to get rid of her? There would have been no need to risk a life sentence for nothing.'

'I suppose you're right,' Eve said.

'Oh God,' Alison said, 'my aunt's coming over.'

Eve groaned. She knew Betty would want to talk about the previous evening and Paul's attack on her. She wanted to put it behind her. Paul had apologised and she had accepted and that was that. She didn't want to discuss it further. However, she was surprised when Betty spoke.

'How are you, Eve? Don and I were concerned about you last night.'

'Oh, I'm fine, thank you. No damage done.'

Why is she being nice? Something's up, I'm sure of it, Betty thought. She said aloud, 'He seems such a nice chap, but you never know, do you? Did you — '

'Everything all right here?' Don said, interrupting his wife.

'Yes, thank you,' Eve replied, wondering what Betty had been going to say. However, she could see that Betty wasn't going to continue. Something was up with those two.

'There you go, Eve — a nice large gin and tonic,' David said, giving her a kiss on the cheek.

Eve glanced at Betty, but she wasn't even looking at them. In fact she was staring at Lucy and Kevin. Had she heard about the police visiting them? Then Eve looked at Don, who was keeping a close eye on Betty. That was it. It suddenly dawned on Eve that he had told her not to interfere. At last Don had stood up to that obnoxious wife of his! However, Eve was certain it wouldn't last long and Betty would be back to her normal nagging self. Or would she? Perhaps Betty might like a more domineering husband. Not that she looked particularly enamoured with him now.

Lucy was downing her third glass of wine. She'd had one before she'd left home and she'd had another very quickly when she'd got to the party. She was sure people were staring at them. Somebody must have seen the police arrive at their house. This was awful. She wished they hadn't come; but if they hadn't, it would have looked suspicious. Who could have told the police? She looked around the room. Ken and Jan were busy behind the bar, and she thought it wouldn't have been them. They barely knew them apart from coming into the Black Cat. Of course, anyone in the room could have seen Kevin go into Jennifer's house that one night he slept with her and suddenly remembered it, thinking it suspicious.

Lucy went up to the bar and got

another glass of wine. She was both bored and tense. Kevin was talking to his brother and just ignoring her as usual. As she walked towards the food, she saw Eve and Jane chatting and stopped suddenly. There was something at the back of her mind concerning Eve, but she couldn't quite remember what it was. She went and got a plate and piled it up with sandwiches and little pies. She was already feeling quite drunk and thought she'd better eat something. She didn't want to say something she'd regret. She often would say such stupid things when she'd had one too many.

Lucy went down and sat at a table and started eating, but she couldn't stop drinking her wine. Paul came up and asked her if she was okay and gave her another glass of wine, saying Kevin would be back in a minute. They were having a discussion about repairing his car. Lucy smiled.

'I'm fine on my own. Tell Kevin not to bother to rush back.'

Paul, however, was a bit worried. He'd seen Lucy before when she was drunk and it could go either way. Sometimes she was lots of fun, but at others she was really evil. He decided to tell Kevin to go and see to his wife.

Having finished her fourth glass of wine, she started on the one Paul had brought. Then she saw Eve getting a plate of food and it clicked. Eve had been coming out of the bathroom the previous night when she and Kevin had been discussing Jennifer. She could have been there for ages and heard everything. That was it. Eve was the one who had told the police. She got up, but found she felt a little wobbly. Steadying herself, she walked towards Eve.

'It was you, wasn't it?' she hissed. 'You told the police. You were listening to my conversation with my husband.'

Eve didn't know what to say. She couldn't deny it, but she didn't want to admit guilt. However, before she could say anything Lucy shouted out, 'You, madam, are a snoop. That's what you are. Neither I nor my husband killed Jennifer, I'll have you know.'

The whole room went silent and Kevin rushed over to Lucy. 'There, there, dear. Of course we didn't,' he said, guiding her away to a chair. She flopped down, looking quite sick. 'I'm sorry, everybody,' Kevin said. 'We've had a slightly bad day. 'I think I'll take my wife home.'

Paul went over and helped him get Lucy up and they took her out of the bar. As soon as they left, everybody started talking amongst themselves.

David went over to Eve. 'What did she say to you?'

'She accused me of going to the police, which of course I did.'

'You did nothing more than tell them what Kevin and Lucy said.'

'I know, but I wish I hadn't.'

'It was the correct thing to do, Eve. The police have a right to investigate them.'

'I suppose so, but I'm a bit scared now.'

'Don't be. They wouldn't dare do anything, not now everyone knows it was you who went to the police.'

'Interfering again,' Betty said, coming up to Eve.

The old Betty's back, I see! thought Eve.

'No she's not,' David remarked immediately. 'She didn't want to go to the police, but I told her to. She overheard something that could be relevant to the case and it was her duty to inform the police.'

Betty looked peeved. It was turning out to be a particularly awful day for her. She was glad the year was at an end.

'Now, everybody,' Ken shouted, banging on the bar. 'Let's all try and get back into the New Year's Eve spirit. The band's about to start playing, so everybody get a drink and some food and have a dance. Let's try and forget about the murder tonight.'

'I think that's a very good idea,' Eve whispered to David.

David could hardly believe it. Eve

had suggested forgetting about the murder. Could life get any better? Unfortunately it was destined to get worse before it was going to improve.

14

A couple of days went by and things in the village settled down. No further progress was made in the case of Jennifer Anderson's murder, or at least nobody heard that anything new had been discovered. There weren't any more arrests and Eve wondered if the police had simply given up. Her faith in them was wavering again.

David was watching Eve like a hawk, and with Alison and Robert still staying with them, there wasn't much she could do to seek out the murderer. Although she had more or less decided to let the police solve the case, boredom was setting in and she was beginning to change her mind about searching for the killer. Life as an amateur detective sounded glamorous again and she had conveniently forgotten about being poisoned. Of course she didn't want to lose David, but Eve had become as complacent as before and thought he would find it impossible to live without her.

David will always return to me, whatever I do! She smiled to herself.

Robert had known Eve for a long time and could see she was getting restless. He was slightly concerned about what she might get up to after he and Alison returned to England on January the fourth. Robert wasn't quite as sure as Eve that David would stay with her through thick and thin. She had tried his patience to the limit this Christmas season, and if Paul hadn't attacked her, they might never have reunited.

The day before, Alison and Robert were due to go home; they had taken their hosts out to Rethymnon for the day in an attempt to distract Eve from thoughts of Jennifer and her murder. After visiting the monastery of Arkadi, not many kilometres south of the town, they had gone into Rethymnon for a delicious lunch in an authentic taverna situated in the harbour.

Eve had a great interest in history and thoroughly enjoyed the visit to Arkadi, fascinated that in 1866 the monastery there had played a very important part in Cretan resistance against the Ottoman occupation. David was more than happy to see she was totally absorbed in something other than murder.

Surprisingly, this day of normality had almost brought Eve back to her senses. She was now simply relieved that David had come back to her. He had been right — she would have been stupid to carry on looking for the killer. This one was even worse than Phyllis. Eve had barely done anything of any note and he or she had already tried to do away with her.

'So what do you think, Eve?' Robert asked when they were all relaxing at home later that day having a drink.

'Sorry, what?'

'You were miles away,' David commented. 'Not thinking about the murder, I hope.' He was still worried that she might get her passion back for being the next Poirot or Miss Marple.

'I was, actually.' David's face fell, but she quickly reassured him. 'But don't worry. I was thinking how right you were. I should keep well clear of this killer. He or she is ruthless.'

David breathed a sigh of relief.

'So what were you saying, Robert?' Eve asked.

'I was suggesting we all went on a tour together of some of the other Greek islands this summer.'

'What about Portia?' Eve asked, stroking her dog.

Portia was lying at her feet, happy as ever.

'I'm sure Annie will look after her, Eve,' David said.

'Okay,' Eve replied, slightly reluctantly. She had left Portia with David while she had been in England, but she had still been concerned about her. For such a tough woman, she worried quite unnecessarily about her dog. Yes, Portia missed her, but as long as she was fed and had a cuddle, Portia would be content while Eve was away.

The doorbell went and everybody looked at Eve. 'I'm not expecting anyone. Will you get it, darling?' she asked, looking at David plaintively.

He nodded. He knew he shouldn't be at her beck and call this much, but she could be very persuasive when she was in such an agreeable mood. He still couldn't believe she wasn't interested in the murder anymore.

David went to answer the door, but his heart sank when he saw Paul standing there.

'Yes?' David said abruptly. Paul was the last person he wanted to see. David was still angry about his attack on Eve, but for some reason Eve had forgiven him and he couldn't understand why. Did she have a soft spot for him? He had never thought Paul was seriously interested in Eve and believed he was just teasing her when he flirted, but now he wasn't so sure. Was Paul trying to lure Eve away from him? David knew he was being insecure, but he couldn't help it. Eve was beautiful, confident and successful. She was a great catch. However, he didn't realise that he was also a particularly handsome man, with a record of many significant achievements behind him.

'I'm sorry to disturb you,' Paul said nervously, knowing David's opinion of him. 'Do you mind if I have a word with you all?'

'Fine. Come in,' David said, not intending to waste words on him.

Paul and David walked into the sitting room, surprising everyone. Eve was pleased Paul had popped in now that they were friends again, but she did wonder why he'd come and was concerned about David's mood. He looked very grim, but she wasn't going to be rude. She jumped up. 'Have a seat, Paul. And a drink?'

'Oh, I don't want to put you out.'

'Don't be silly.'

'A whisky then?' Paul asked tentatively.

'David? And you might as well top up all our drinks.'

David gritted his teeth. Now he had

to serve that man. However, he couldn't make a scene. He'd look stupid and jealous.

Once they were all seated with their drinks replenished, Paul began to speak. 'I wanted to apologise for my sister-in-law, Lucy. She does feel terrible about her behaviour on New Year's Eve.'

'Then why didn't she come herself?' Robert asked.

'She's a proud woman.'

'I suppose she's still not happy about Eve going to the police?' David asked.

'Well, she says she's innocent, so she's naturally annoyed.'

'So she's not really apologising at all; it's you, isn't it? You just wanted an excuse to come here.' His voice was tinged with anger.

'Why would I want an excuse?'

Eve was getting anxious. David was about to make a fool of himself and she had to do something, so she butted in quickly. 'Now come on, you two; don't argue. Paul's probably had an awful time with his brother and sister-in-law. I mean, Lucy was in an awful state when we last saw her. It must have taken her ages to calm down.'

Paul nodded vigorously. 'Yes, it took us the rest of the evening to get her back to normal.'

'I was in two minds about whether to go to the police, Paul, I really was. David, Alison and Robert persuaded me to tell them. I mean the evidence I had didn't mean either Kevin or Lucy killed Jennifer. I think David was worried I might start snooping on my own if I didn't tell the police what I knew.'

'I totally understand, Eve,' Paul agreed. 'Neither Kevin nor Lucy was arrested, so the police haven't got the evidence to put either of them in jail for Jennifer's murder. Both of them have a tendency to overreact to everything.'

'You're very different to your brother, Paul,' Eve remarked.

'Well, I was adopted, so it's not surprising I suppose.'

'Really? You seem close though.'

'We are — well, we were. Gradually

over the years Lucy's come between us.'

David was getting fed up. Eve and Paul seemed to be having a conversation between themselves, but he couldn't think of anything to say to join in with them. He looked at Robert and made a face at him. He wanted him to say something to get rid of Paul.

'Well, we've had yet another exciting holiday,' Robert commented, not knowing what to say to help David. 'Though the one consolation is that at least nobody tried to kill me this time!'

Everybody laughed and the ice was broken. David was relieved. They chatted a little more about Alison and Robert's holiday and then Paul decided to leave. He knew David didn't want him there.

'Well, I'm glad he's gone,' David said as soon as Paul had left.

'You weren't very pleasant to him,' Eve replied.

'Well, he's keen on you.'

'Nonsense. It's your imagination.'

Alison and Robert looked at each other, knowing that an argument was about to start. 'Come on, you two,' Alison said severely. 'We'll have none of that. It's time to get ready for our farewell dinner in Chania. We want to have a nice time on our last night here. Can you promise us that?'

Eve and David looked at each other, feeling well and truly told off. They nodded and headed upstairs to get ready. Robert shook his head, wondering again what would happen when they left Crete.

* * *

That same evening James went to answer his door at eight o'clock. Standing there was a slightly nervous Jane. She was wearing another of Eve's dresses — not that she would tell James that it wasn't hers. Eve had promised to take her into Chania to buy some new clothes in a couple of days' time and she was looking forward to it. She could certainly afford a new and more glamorous wardrobe now that she had inherited all that money from her father.

My God, she looks stunning again, thought James. *And to think, when I first met her I couldn't imagine taking her to important business functions. Now she would fit in perfectly in any situation*. He said aloud, 'You look beautiful again tonight, darling. Come in. Dinner's almost ready.'

Jane was looking forward to the evening. James hadn't cooked for her before and she had no idea if he had any culinary skills, but she imagined he was an excellent chef. James was proficient in everything he did; he was quite the perfect man.

As she entered the house, a wonderful aroma wafted over her and she was filled with anticipation. 'Dinner smells wonderful, darling,' she commented.

'I hope you enjoy it. I absolutely love to cook. But let me take your coat first.'

Jane slipped off her coat while trying to look calm and collected, but she was shaking. However, James didn't notice and could only see this beautiful young woman standing before him. She had on a light-green sleeveless dress which fitted her perfectly. It was lucky that she was exactly the same size as Eve.

Jane had also brought a little black shiny cardigan with her in case it got cold later in the evening, but James always put the central heating on high after dark. He hated the cold. He was only wearing a shirt without a jacket this evening and Jane didn't think she would have to use her cardigan either.

Jane had left her hair loose and James imagined running his fingers through it later that evening and slipping her dress off. He knew he had to stop thinking about what was going to happen in a few hours' time. He had to concentrate on the present and couldn't let dinner spoil. James was a great perfectionist and refused to let anything he did go wrong. 'Come into the lounge,' he said. 'A drink before dinner?'

'Yes, please. A gin and tonic?'

'Of course.'

They sat together for a little while

before James went back into the kitchen. He left some music on for Jane and she felt so happy that she almost got up and danced on her own.

A little later on, James called her into the dining room for the first course. Jane was impressed when she saw how beautifully the table had been laid. There was a pure white tablecloth on the table, and in the large but delicate wine glasses were white cloth napkins. James led Jane to the table and pulled out a chair for her. 'The first course is seafood crepes,' he said.

'They look absolutely delicious, James,' Jane replied.

James poured the wine, a Vouvray — a light French wine — and smiled. 'I hope you enjoy the crepes, and the wine. It goes very well with seafood.'

Jane was already impressed with both his knowledge of wine and the presentation of the food. They started eating and Jane couldn't believe how tasty the crepes were. James was a talented man. Was there no end to his skills? 'These crepes are delicious. They could be so heavy and filling, but they're not. They're light, and the seafood is perfectly cooked. You're an excellent chef, James.'

'Thank you, darling.' He looked pleased, but not surprised. James was a man who was used to being successful in everything he did.

He allowed a decent break between the first and main courses and poured them another glass of wine. 'Oh, I shall be getting tipsy,' Jane said, laughing.

'That's all right. It doesn't matter to let your hair down once in a while.' He reached over and kissed her. She felt herself trembling with desire. James was handsome and talented, not to mention successful. She couldn't believe her luck in meeting him, but then a cold shiver ran through her. Although the police had released him, he wasn't totally off the hook for the murder of his aunt. There simply wasn't enough evidence. He could still have killed her.

I'm just being silly, she thought. *Why would he want to kill her? She didn't have that much money, did she? James is rich in his own right, so her money would be a drop in the ocean. It wouldn't have been worth the risk of going to jail, would it?*

'What's wrong, Jane?' James asked. 'You seem miles away.'

'Nothing's wrong, darling,' Jane replied, knowing she was lying just a tad. 'I was just thinking how different this Christmas turned out to be. I was expecting to be alone and quite miserable, yet look what's happened.'

'It's been completely different to what I expected too, but I couldn't be happier.'

'Me either.' *Everything will be fine, I'm sure*, thought Jane. *How could somebody like James ever kill anyone? He's not the sort. He's a gentleman*.

'Now for the next course,' James continued. 'It's rack of lamb.'

'Wonderful,' Jane said, the smells already wafting in from the kitchen.

James opened a bottle of Pinot Noir to go with the lamb, but Jane was drinking very slowly now. She was worried that she would get drunk. Jane didn't drink a lot normally and didn't want to lose control.

For dessert, James presented a rich chocolate torte and they had small glasses of dessert wine to go with it. Jane was feeling full and her head was spinning from all the alcohol. She realised she hadn't been drinking slowly enough.

'Are you all right?' James asked.

'A little too much food and wine, I think.'

'Go and sit down on the sofa and I'll tidy up.'

'Let me help you, James.'

'I won't hear of it, Jane. Let the food settle and I'll join you shortly.'

'You're a marvellous host,' Jane said, kissing him on the cheek. He grinned as he started to clear the table.

Half an hour later, James came and sat down on the sofa next to Jane. She was fast asleep and he kissed her lightly. She woke up with a start. 'Oh, I'm so sorry. I dropped off.'

'That's all right, darling. I shouldn't

have woken you. You looked so beautiful and peaceful lying there.'

'Thank you. I actually feel wide awake now. That nap did me the world of good.'

'I'm glad,' he said, stroking her cheek. 'My God, you are stunning, Jane. I'm a lucky man.' He brought his lips to hers and Jane felt herself trembling with desire again. She didn't want the moment to end, all her fears of him killing his aunt evaporating into the night. As their lips parted, she couldn't hold back any longer.

'I love you, James. I know we only met a few days ago, but I feel as if I've known you for ever. I know I can't expect the same feelings from you.'

'Why not? From the moment we met, I knew you were special. I don't give my heart away easily, Jane, but I will admit I am falling in love with you.'

'Oh James,' she said, throwing her arms around him. 'This has been the perfect Christmas.'

'Yes it has, darling. Yes it has.'

15

At about eleven the following morning, Eve and David returned home, having taken Alison and Robert to the airport to catch their flight back to England. Eve collapsed on the sofa as soon as they got in.

'It's been lovely having guests, but it is nice to have the place to ourselves again.'

'Yes it is, darling,' David replied, sitting down next to her. He put his arm around Eve and then gently kissed her. 'It's been a traumatic holiday season, hasn't it?' he remarked once their lips had parted.

'You could say that,' Eve sighed. 'I know you're talking about the murder, but I must admit that I'm quite looking forward to a rest after all this partying.'

'You, tired of partying? I don't believe it!' They both laughed, but suddenly Eve looked serious. 'What's wrong, Eve?'

'I was thinking of Jennifer. Do you think the police are still doing anything to find her killer? She might not have been a nice woman, but she deserves justice.'

'I have no idea what's happening, Eve. You're not thinking of searching for the murderer again, are you?' he asked wearily.

David had naturally been concerned about this. He had wondered if once Alison and Robert had gone home, Eve might get bored and want to look for the killer again.

'No, of course not. I'd have absolutely no idea where to start anyway.'

'Good.'

'And of course I wouldn't want you leaving me again.'

'I don't think I could ever leave you, Eve. I was too worried about you when I was gone last time. But I will be really angry if you do start all that nonsense again.'

Eve sighed for a second time. She did love David, but why wasn't he interested in getting involved in more exciting and adventurous things? Eve thoroughly enjoyed taking risks, thinking how much more exhilarating it made life.

'Right, I'm going upstairs to get on with my writing,' David stated. 'My agent's given me a deadline and I've not got a lot of time left. I hope you won't be too bored without me.'

'I'll be fine. Don't worry; I won't do anything reckless. See you later.'

Eve lay back on the sofa, feeling a bit tired. Portia jumped up and put her head on her lap. Eve thought about the murder, not really coming up with any new ideas. She began dozing off, but then sat up with a start, remembering something Paul had said the night before. He had told them he was adopted.

What if Jennifer Anderson had been his real mother and he had killed her because she had abandoned him? He had a temper, as she well knew. However, the murder had been planned and wasn't committed in a fit of rage. Perhaps Paul had thought about killing her from the day he found out she was his birth mother. He could possibly have asked Jennifer to move to Crete so they could get to know each other and then pretended to get on with her. Then on Christmas Eve he had gone over to Jennifer's house, taking the dessert wine as a gift. Little did she know that it was laced with strychnine and was going to be the last thing she would ever drink.

Eve knew she couldn't go to the police with this story. After all, she had only thought of it herself and it could easily be completely untrue. What was she to do? Perhaps she should go and talk to James. He might know if his aunt had had an illegitimate child that she'd given up for adoption.

Eve then wondered if she should go and tell David that she was popping out. *No, I'd better not. He'll be busy working, and besides, he doesn't want me interfering in the murder anyway — not that this is really interfering, but he would still be angry. However, he did say he wouldn't leave me again, so I've nothing to lose. I'll go and talk to James. Nothing will probably come of it, so David will never need to know.*

Eve went and put on her jacket. Portia looked up expectantly, but Eve decided to leave her dog at home, remembering when Phyllis almost killed her pet by giving her rat poison. She had decided never to take Portia with her whenever she did anything connected with murder.

As Eve strolled through the village, she nearly turned round and went back home. This was probably a waste of time. Paul probably wasn't Jennifer's son, and even if he was, why would she tell James? After all, they didn't get on.

Eve was disappointed in herself. She'd had much better ideas during the summer murders. What had happened to her brilliant mind? However, in the end, she decided to keep walking. What else was she going to do today anyway?

Arriving at her destination, Eve saw that James had parked his car outside his house and right next to it was Paul's. Her heart started beating faster. Perhaps her theory was right after all. However, Eve's first inclination was to run away.

What is wrong with me? I didn't used to be this timid. But it does seem strange that Paul is visiting James. Come on, I've got to pull myself together and find out what's going on.

Eve rang the doorbell, but there was no reply. She rang again, but still nobody came to the door. She knew James was at home, so why wasn't he answering?

Something fishy is going on, and I'm not leaving.

Eve started banging at the door and finally James appeared.

'What on earth is going on?' he asked, looking flustered and quite angry.

Eve realised she hadn't planned what to say. 'Err, I was looking for Paul and saw his car outside,' she said loudly, in case he was close by and could hear her.

'He's not here.'

'Well, that's strange. Why would he park outside your house then? It seems very odd.'

'I have no idea, Eve,' James replied, sounding annoyed. He wanted her to go, but she was rooted to the spot.

'How was your dinner with Jane last night?'

'Lovely. Now, if you'll excuse me.'

Suddenly there was a bang from the sitting room. Both of them looked towards the room.

'What was that?' Eve asked.

'I have no idea. I'm sure it's nothing important,' James replied, sweat starting to run down his forehead.

Another small bang followed and Eve leapt towards the sitting room door before James could stop her. When she opened it, she gasped. Both Jane and Paul were sitting on the sofa, hands and feet tied up and their mouths covered with tape. A couple of ornaments were on the floor, obviously knocked down by Paul from the table next to him.

Suddenly Eve felt an arm around her neck and a gun in her back.

'You should have just left when you had the chance, Eve,' James hissed. 'Now you'll have to join your friends on the settee.'

Eve felt sick. Why hadn't she listened to David? He always knew best, yet she continually went off and did her own thing. He would be mad with her this time. That was, if she came out alive.

* * *

Jane had woken up late that same morning and was surprised to see it was well after ten thirty. She felt in the bed for James, but he wasn't there. She knew he had work to do, so she had expected him to get up early. He had told her to have a lie-in the previous night, so she was sure he wouldn't mind her being in bed so late.

Jane got up and went to have a bath

and do her make-up. As she came out of the bathroom, James came in with a breakfast tray. It was beautifully set out with flowers, fresh juice, cereal, boiled eggs, toast, croissants and marmalade.

'Oh James, you shouldn't have,' she said, delighted nevertheless.

James put the tray down, then took her in his arms and kissed her passionately, holding her close. 'Yes, I should have,' he said moments later. 'You deserve it. Unfortunately, I'm afraid I must make a few phone calls to the UK now that it's after nine over there, so enjoy this and I'll see you a bit later.

'Okay, darling.'

Jane sat down to indulge in her special breakfast. James was completely spoiling her and she didn't mind one bit. Could life get any better?

* * *

About forty minutes later Jane was full up, having thoroughly enjoyed her wonderful breakfast, and wondered if it would be all right to go downstairs. She didn't know why she was nervous. She had spent a night of passion with James, so she shouldn't be uneasy with him; but she was on edge, not wanting to disturb him if he was still working.

I'm being silly. Why aren't I completely relaxed with the man I love?

Finally Jane got up the courage to go downstairs. She went and put the tray in the kitchen and then went towards the sitting room. She was about to open the door when she heard voices. One was James, but she couldn't quite make out who the other person was.

'I shall be contesting the will,' James said abruptly.

'It won't do you much good.'

'You're Jennifer's bastard child. She didn't even want you. She was totally ashamed of what she had done and that you were the result of it.'

Jane gasped. Jennifer had a son. Who was it? She still couldn't tell who the other voice belonged to.

'She changed her mind about me. We were getting on well.'

'Well, you're not having her money,' James continued.

'Why are you so concerned about her money, James? She didn't have that much. You're a rich man and her cash is a drop in the ocean to you.'

'I had to put up with her all my life. You didn't deserve the money and I'm having it,' James remarked stubbornly.

'As I said, I don't think you'll win.'

Oh my goodness, Jane gasped again. *That's Paul. He's Jennifer's son. He must have killed her for the money.*

'Well,' James said harshly, 'there are other ways.'

What's he going on about? Jane wondered.

'Now James, put that away,' she heard Paul say. 'Look, we can discuss this man to man; there's no need for violence.'

Jane stumbled against the door and wanted to run upstairs and hide, but she was frozen in fear.

'Jane, are you out there?' she heard James call. 'If you are, come in here.'

Jane wasn't able to do anything but obey him. When she opened the door, she saw Paul standing completely still with James holding a gun at him. In that one moment all her hopes and dreams disappeared.

'I'm sorry, Jane,' James said coldly. 'I wish you hadn't come downstairs and seen this. Then everything could have remained as it was between us. Now I'm going to have to get rid of you as well, I'm afraid.'

'I thought you loved me, James,' she said, tears beginning to fall.

'I did — I do — but I'm not going to jail,' James replied. 'Now, get over there.'

'But why, James — why did you kill her? I thought you had money?'

At that moment, the doorbell rang and James grabbed Jane and threw her on the settee.

'Don't you dare make a sound,' he said harshly, as he first tied up Paul's hands and legs and taped up his mouth, before doing the same to Jane. Paul looked at her. She was weeping and all he wanted to do was put his arms around her, but he couldn't. He had known all along that James was no good for her, and now he had broken her heart. If they ever got out of this mess, he would try and mend that heart of hers if he could . . . and if she would let him.

The person outside was now banging at the door very loudly.

Who is that at the door? Please don't let them give up, Paul prayed.

* * *

Eve was now tied up as well, but James had run out of tape. 'Now, keep your mouth shut, Eve,' he spoke severely. 'I won't hesitate to shoot you.'

Eve was certain he wouldn't, but she wondered if he really would have the nerve to kill all three of them.

'Before your untimely arrival, Eve,

Jane asked why I killed my aunt if I had so much money. To tell the truth, I also have a lot of debts. I like to gamble — the big league, of course. However, these debts have been mounting up, so I had to do something about it.

'I lied to you all about my relationship with my aunt. Jennifer and I actually got on very well. It was my mother I didn't get on with. Jennifer promised me that she was going to leave me everything in her wills, both here and in England. I was her only relative . . . or so I thought. I didn't plan to kill her. I actually came here before Christmas to ask if I could borrow some money to help pay off the debts, but she didn't have much to hand. She still had the house in England and had spent all her cash on the house here, but she said once she sold the house in the UK she would lend me some money. I couldn't wait that long, so she had to go.

'What that bitch hadn't told me was that her son . . . ' He paused, the anger rising again. 'I can barely say that word . . . Her son had contacted her. That was the reason she moved here, to be near him.' James pointed at Paul, his finger shaking. 'Paul had found out who she was and had gone to see her in England. They had got on well and she moved here to get to know him. Apparently you didn't tell anyone that she was your mother, did you, Paul? Not even your brother or sister-in-law. And she didn't bother to tell me she'd changed her wills. If she had, she would be alive today. There would have been no point killing her. But I thought with you dead, Paul, I'd inherit everything after all.'

'How do you possibly think you'll get away with it, James? You'll have to kill all of us,' Eve said. She was trembling, but was determined not let it show. She had been in these situations before and got out of them.

'Don't you think I know that?' James snapped at Eve. 'Oh, Jane, why did you have to find us? I would only have had to get rid of Paul. It would have been so much easier.'

Jane bowed her head, still weeping. Both Paul and Eve wanted to put their arms around her and give her some comfort.

Eve studied James. He looked anxious. Perhaps he wouldn't go through with it. Three people were a lot to kill and she didn't think he was a seasoned murderer. He had only been expecting to kill Paul, but now he had to kill two women as well and he was in love with one of them. Eve had no doubt that he did love Jane, but he was in a mess now. The only alternative he had was to lock them up somewhere where they wouldn't be found for some time, and get away from the island. He would have to forget about the money and go on the run. Would he want to do that?

James sat down, gun pointing at the three of them. *What am I to do?* he thought. *Can I really kill all of them? What did that Phyllis do? She put Eve in the basement and tried to set the house on fire, but it didn't work. I could set a fire better than her, but I haven't got a basement, so I'd have to do it in here. Plus it's daylight and I could be seen, or the fire could be discovered long before they're dead. It's over, isn't it?*

James sat there thinking while Eve watched him carefully. *He doesn't know what to do. There's too many of us. Perhaps he'll cave in and give himself up.*

Paul was thinking almost the same thing. James hadn't planned to kill all three of them, but perhaps he would go crazy with fear and shoot them anyway. Then he would drive off, hoping to disappear somewhere in the mountains.

James got up and checked the locks on the windows and doors. They all watched him and Jane started sobbing again. Paul moved closer and tried to rub his arm against hers. He so wanted to give her a hug, but that touch was enough to calm her.

'I'm locking you in here for a moment, but I'll be back soon, so don't get any ideas,' James said as he left the room.

'Oh, I'm so sorry about this, Jane. I feel it's all my fault,' Eve said. 'I should never have encouraged you to go out with James. We should have remained on guard after the first time he was arrested, but we didn't believe he was guilty.'

'I did,' Paul said, having managed to get the tape off his mouth. 'The tape wasn't very strong, Jane. Keep trying to move your mouth and it might come off.' She nodded.

'Yes,' Eve said to Paul, 'you were the only sensible one.'

'Well, I don't know. I wasn't sure if he did kill my mother. I knew they were close; she told me that, so I thought it strange he told Jane he didn't like her. I was worried the police might suspect me if they knew I was her long-lost son, so I kept my mouth shut. Bit stupid really.'

'Perhaps; but you're right. You would have been a suspect, probably their major suspect.'

'There, done it,' Jane said, finally managing to get the tape off her mouth.

'How are you, Jane?' Paul asked. 'I know this must be awful for you.'

'It's not turning out to be the best day of my life. I can't believe I fell in love with such a monster. And you warned me, Paul. Oh why didn't I take any notice of you? Why?'

'James bowled you over,' Paul said sadly. 'I was hoping to do that, but unfortunately it was he who captivated you.'

'Thank you for trying to comfort me a little while ago, Paul, despite being tied up. I really appreciate it.'

'You're welcome. I wish you hadn't come in and seen this, but then James might have got rid of me and you'd have been left with a killer. Who knows when he might have struck again?'

Jane smiled. *How sweet. He's only thinking of me, not of himself.* Why had she fallen for such an evil man? Then she remembered the previous evening and the wonderful meal. It had been a perfect night. James had been both passionate and tender and she could hardly believe that he was a cold-blooded killer.

'So what are we going to do, Paul?' Eve asked, feeling they were wasting time.

'I don't know if there is anything we can do,' Paul replied. 'I've been wriggling my hands and feet, but the ropes have been tied much too tightly.'

'Mine have been too,' Eve said, while Jane just nodded.

James came back into the room carrying three syringes.

'No, James,' Jane cried out. 'Please don't hurt us.'

'I see you've got your tape off. And you too, Paul. Well, it was the end of the roll and probably not sticky enough. Never mind. I'm going to check your ropes now and I don't want you to move. Do you understand?'

They all nodded. Eve decided there was no point begging for mercy. James was going to do what he wanted, but she somehow had a feeling he wasn't going to kill them. As he wouldn't be able to get Jennifer's money now, there was no point killing an extra three people. He was probably going to cut his losses and run, but whatever was in those syringes would probably knock them out for a long time.

'Right, you first, Paul.' James stated, completely without emotion.

'You'll never get the money now, James; you do know that, don't you?' Paul said. 'And I don't know how you thought you'd get it if you shot me.'

'I wasn't going to shoot you. I know that wouldn't have got me the money. I was just trying to show you who was boss, but then everything went wrong. This really is your fault, Jane, coming into the sitting room when you did. You spoilt my plans. I'm not too happy with you, but I refuse to get caught and put in jail.'

'Please don't kill me. Last night was wonderful. I thought . . . '

'Don't think about last night. That time is over. You ended it, not me. I should kill you, my darling, but I'm not one to take revenge. You will meet the same fate as the others.'

I was right; he's not going to murder us, thought Eve. *Or is he lulling us into a false sense of security?*

'And you, Eve Masters, always poking you nose in where it's not wanted. You should listen to David and stop playing detective.'

Eve felt herself going red. James might be a bastard, but he was right. Why hadn't she listened to David? If she lived through this and he forgave her, she would never ever interfere in anybody's life again. Of that she was certain.

James moved towards Paul with the first syringe. Paul sat completely still while James injected him. He knew there was no point struggling. Next he went to Jane. What a pity. She was beautiful and she did everything he wanted her to. She would have made a perfect wife. Jane started weeping again and James, refusing to look at her face, injected the syringe into her thin arm. Then he went to Eve. She had decided to act like Paul and not say a word, but in the end she couldn't help herself.

'You really are a nasty piece of work, aren't you, James? It was bad enough killing your aunt, but what you did to Jane beggars belief.'

'You had to have the last word, didn't you, Eve? You couldn't just sit there and take it like Paul. I don't know how David puts up with you.'

'Oh shut up and get on with it,' she replied. 'It'll be worth it not to have to see your face again.' However, she was trembling, hoping that it was just something that would make them sick and not kill them.

James sat and watched. Eve didn't say another word to him, but she couldn't believe he could sit there expressionless, especially looking at Jane, the woman he had professed his love to. Jane had moved closer to Paul and leant her head against him for comfort, but Eve saw no change in James's expression — not that Eve felt she was doing it to make him jealous. She was just scared.

Jane was affected by whatever was in the syringe first. She felt sick and dizzy. *Oh no, I'm going to die*, she thought. Then she felt something running out of her nose and noticed drops of blood on her clothes. Tears started to fall, but she wanted them to stop. She didn't want James to see how vulnerable she was.

James tried not to look at her. Visions of the previous night flashed through his mind. Why couldn't he be completely cold-hearted? Life would be much easier. *And why did Paul have to turn up so quickly this morning?* he asked himself.

James had phoned his lawyer in London about Jennifer's will and had been informed that Paul was the sole beneficiary as he was Jennifer's son. It had been a total shock. James had been straight on the phone to Paul telling him they needed to talk. He hadn't expected Paul to come straight over. If he hadn't, James would have been able to form a plan and none of this need have happened. Yes, he could have planted strychnine somewhere in Paul's house and engineered for it to be discovered. He wasn't sure how, but he would have worked it out. James was nothing if not resourceful. Then Paul would have been arrested for Jennifer's murder and he and Jane would have lived happily ever after. But he had to forget these thoughts and concentrate on the future. He had to forget about the money and about going back to England. The people he owed cash to would be on his back straightaway if he returned to the UK.

He was jolted out of these thoughts by Jane being sick. Paul now had his head on his knees so it didn't look as if he felt too good either. Eve was retching and it seemed as if she too would be sick at any minute. He glanced at Jane and it seemed as if she had passed out.

That was very quick, but then she is quite fragile.

He turned towards Paul, not wanting to look at Jane anymore. Paul, who was as white as a sheet, tried to get up. With his legs tied up, he naturally fell over and started coughing before he too was sick. Eve felt her head would explode and the pains in her abdomen were getting worse. For a moment she wished she would pass out like Jane, but then changed her mind, thinking she might never wake up again. However, Jane wasn't dead. Eve could see her chest going up and down. There was still hope.

Paul, lying on the ground, felt his vision go blurry and he shut his eyes. He was tired anyway. His stomach hurt and he wished he could go to sleep. If he died, he died. Anything would be better than this pain.

James got up and looked at them. Jane was definitely out and Paul seemed to be. He kicked him and Paul moaned, but didn't say anything. He went over to Eve, who stared at him.

'Well, I'll be off then,' he said to her. 'I'm sure it won't be too long before you're found.'

'You won't get away with it,' she whispered, unable to speak any louder.

'Perhaps, perhaps not.'

James turned and left the room, locking the door behind him. He picked up a suitcase he had left in the hall and got into his car.

* * *

Around five that afternoon, David came downstairs. He had been totally engrossed in his work and hadn't realised what the time was. He saw Portia standing at the door, wanting to go into the garden. He let her out, but thought it was a little odd. Eve tended to walk the dog for about an hour around three thirty, so why did Portia want to go out again so soon; and where was Eve?

'Eve,' he called out a couple of times.

There was no reply, so he looked outside. Her car was in the driveway, so she couldn't have gone far. Perhaps she'd popped out to the local shop.

David went and made a coffee, but when Eve hadn't returned half an hour later he started to become concerned. It would be getting dark soon and she wouldn't normally go for a walk alone in the fading light. He told himself he was being silly, but with the murder still being unsolved and Eve being Eve, anything could have happened.

David picked up the phone and tried Eve's mobile. When she didn't answer, he tried another number.

'Annie, hello. I was wondering if you'd seen Eve this afternoon.'

'No, I'm afraid not. Why? Have you lost her?'

'I've been so involved in writing my novel that I lost all track of time; and when I came downstairs, she wasn't here.'

'Oh I'm sure she'll come home soon. She's probably just gone to the shop.'

'You're probably right. Thanks, Annie.'

He tried Jane next, but again there was no reply. David was becoming anxious. Where else could she be? She didn't get on with Betty or Lucy, so there was little chance she would be with either of them.

What was he to do? This didn't feel right to him. She had said she wouldn't get involved in the murder again, but this was Eve he was talking about. She could have suddenly come up with an idea and thrown caution to the wind.

Portia wanted to come back in, so David opened the door, but he couldn't settle. In the end, he grabbed his car keys and decided to drive slowly around the village to see if he could spot Eve.

It took very little time at all and it was a fruitless journey, but David decided to stop at Annie and Pete's before going home.

'You really are worried about her, aren't you?' Annie said, answering the door. 'I must admit, I am too.'

Pete came to the door and stood

behind his wife. 'Have you tried anywhere else?' he asked.

'No; I did ring Jane earlier, but she wasn't at home, nor did she answer her mobile. That made me a little nervous as well.'

'Look, we'll go and see if Betty and Don or Kevin and Lucy have seen her. I know it's unlikely, but it's worth a check. One of them might have been driving and spotted her. You go to Jane's, James's and Paul's.'

'Okay. Thanks for your help. I really appreciate it.'

Betty and Don and Kevin and Lucy lived in the next village. They parted company and David headed first to Jane's house and then to Paul's, both of which he found in darkness.

* * *

Once James had gone, Eve tried to call out to Paul, but she could barely speak. He looked like he'd passed out anyway. She lay back. Her head was spinning and she wished she'd never come out that afternoon. However, she was sure David would find them soon. That was, if he ever stopped writing.

Unfortunately, the time dragged on and nobody came to rescue them. *Damn you, David, stop writing and come and look for me*, Eve begged.

She immediately felt guilty. It wasn't his fault she was in this mess. It was hers. Why hadn't she told David she was going out and where she was heading? Why had she been so stupid? He would probably have stopped her going and she would have been cross with him, but at least she would have been safe.

Eve looked at the others. Jane was still out cold, but finally Paul was stirring. She had been scared of never waking up again and had refused to let herself drop off, doing everything in her power to stay awake.

Paul pulled himself up. 'Eve, are you all right?'

'I feel awful, but at least I'm alive. What about you?'

'Same. My head is throbbing and my stomach aches. God, what did he give us?'

'I dread to think.'

'How's Jane?' Paul asked nervously.

'Still asleep. I didn't pass out; I don't know why. I did desperately try to stay awake though.'

'You've probably got a strong constitution, Eve. You survived all that arsenic, after all. I wonder where James has gone.'

'He's probably trying to get off the island. But even if he does, I expect he'll be caught in Athens. Of course he could have other plans, although I don't know what they could be.'

'If only we could get these ropes off.'

'I wish we could, but they're so tight. I'm sure David will send out a search party for us eventually. He gets so wrapped up in his writing, but he will realise I've gone missing at some point.'

'I hope so. Eve, is there any way you can put on that table light next to you? It's almost dark.'

'I'll try.' The light had a cord with a

switch on it and Eve struggled for about five minutes to turn it on, but she finally managed. However, the effort made her feel nauseous again.

'Thanks, Eve,' Paul said. 'At least we won't have to sit in the dark, plus if anyone comes, they'll think someone's in.'

About half an hour later, the door bell rang and they both jumped. Jane was still out cold.

'Quick, we have to do something,' Eve said.

Both Paul and Eve started shouting, but neither had regained full use of their voices. The door bell rang again and they were sure that whoever it was would go away. As quickly as he was able, Paul slid across the floor, relieved that as in most Greek houses, there wasn't a carpet. Reaching the other end of the room, he knocked down a large marble statue of Zeus which came crashing down with an almighty bang. Paul was lucky not to get hurt, while Eve threw herself on top of Jane to shield her from flying shards of marble.

The noise had the desired effect. David, who was at the door, started ringing and banging, but getting no reply, rushed to the back of the house. Peering into the sitting room, he saw Eve, Paul and Jane and realised they were tied up and unable to let him in. David tried to open the door, but it was locked. As luck would have it, however, it was a new house built by the company John Phillips had owned. He had had a reputation for shoddy workmanship and indeed, this house was not well built and David was easily able to break down the door. He rushed in and hugged Eve before quickly untying all three of them.

'James poisoned us, but we don't know what with. He used a syringe. Jane's still out and I'm really worried about her,' Eve said hurriedly.

She was delighted to see David, but at the moment was more concerned about Jane because she hadn't woken up yet. Eve felt she needed to get to the hospital as soon as possible.

The next thirty minutes were a blur. David rang Pete on his mobile and he and Annie rushed over. Both were shocked to hear what had happened, hardly able to believe James was the murderer. David rang both the police and an ambulance, but being a distance from Chania, they took some time to arrive. Eve started panicking about Jane, although David was also worried about her and Paul. After all, they had been injected with the same poison.

Dimitris Kastrinakis and a couple of other officers were the first to arrive. He was stunned to see the state Eve, Paul and particularly Jane were in. Jane had now been laid down on the settee to make her more comfortable, but she was extremely pale and Paul was pacing up and down, concerned that the ambulance would never arrive. Dimitris, however, thought that all three of them looked like they needed immediate medical attention.

'I'm pleased to see that you're all still

alive. I take it she's still breathing?' Dimitris asked, pointing to Jane on the settee.

Eve nodded, not wanting to say much in case she was given a talking-to for interfering. David hadn't told her off, but at the moment he was relieved she was alive, plus he knew she'd had a traumatic afternoon and had probably thought she was going to die. He didn't want her to be even more stressed than she already was.

'The airports and ports are being informed to look out for James Anderson, but he may already have left. In that case, he will be looked for on all planes and ships leaving Athens.'

'What if he decides to get out of Athens some other way, or stay there?' Paul asked.

'Well, he can't stay in hiding forever. I'm certain we'll find him.'

Eve wasn't so sure, but he probably didn't have that much money.

'So, who was the first to arrive here?' Dimitris asked.

'That would be me,' Paul said and went on to tell him what had happened and how Jane had got involved.

Dimitris indicated to one of his men to write everything down. When Paul had finished talking, he turned towards Eve. 'Now, Miss Masters,' Dimitris continued.

Eve jumped. Now he was going to start on her. *Where on earth is that ambulance?* she asked herself. *I'm feeling dizzy again*.

'Is this really necessary?' David asked. 'Can't you see how ill they all are?'

'Of course I can, sir. Just a brief description of events please, if possible, Miss Masters.'

'Okay. It's fine, David. I'd rather get it over and done with. There's not much to tell anyway.'

Eve went on to explain how she had suspected that Paul was Jennifer's son and didn't know whether to tell the police or not, so she had gone to ask James what he thought. However, she had found Paul and Jane tied up and ended up in the same boat.

As she was finishing, they heard the ambulance arrive. Eve was relieved. Jane needed to get to the hospital and she and Paul had to be checked out as well. She also wanted to end her conversation with Dimitris before he had a go at her. She was surprised he hadn't told her off already.

It wasn't long before the three of them were in the ambulance, and half an hour later they arrived in the hospital. After they had been examined, they were all kept in.

'I'll go home and get your overnight things, darling,' David said. 'Cheer up. Hopefully you won't be here for long.'

'Oh, I'm used to this hospital now,' Eve said, trying to smile. 'I don't feel at all well, so it's for the best. I can't believe you've forgiven me though.'

'Eve, let's not talk about it. I'm sure I'll be very cross when I've got over the shock. You need to get yourself something to do, you know. You're much too intelligent to sit at home doing nothing.'

'I know,' she said, but he could see she was drifting off to sleep.

David kissed the top of her head and went home. When he returned, she was fast asleep, so he gently woke her to tell her he had come back with her things. Eve changed into a nightdress, but said she felt weak and tired so he left her to sleep, hoping this would be the last time that she would ever be in hospital because of her amateur sleuthing. This last incident must have terrified her enough to put her off. He was sure of it.

16

The following morning David was up bright and early to return to the hospital. He had hardly slept, he had been so concerned about Eve. David knew that she had cheated death yet again, but despite having left her a few days previously, albeit for one night, he knew he wouldn't be able to do it again even though she had got involved in the murder enquiries for the umpteenth time. She was a frustrating and difficult woman, but she was exciting and sexy as well and there was never a dull moment with her. David knew he was head over heels in love with Eve. His life had never been the same since she had come into it and he didn't want his dull and boring existence back again.

David got into his car and first picked up Annie and Pete. They also wanted to visit Eve. Annie had been up half the night worrying about her and whether there would be any long-lasting effects from whatever she had been poisoned with.

David and his friends arrived at the hospital around ten and found Eve sitting up in bed. 'How are you darling?' David asked, kissing her.

'I feel a bit better today, though I'm still pretty tired.'

'Have you been told what was in the syringe yet?'

'Unfortunately not, but hopefully they'll know this morning.'

Paul, who was in the ward next to Eve's, came in. Both wards were small, only holding four people. Paul also looked tired, but he too was feeling a bit better than he had done the previous day. 'Good news,' he remarked. 'The doctor said Jane has woken up. They're doing some other tests on her, but we should be able to see her soon.'

'That's a relief,' Eve said. 'I was scared she wouldn't make it.'

Paul nodded, indicating he had

thought exactly the same thing.

A doctor then walked in. 'Miss Masters, I have the results of your tests.'

'I'm Paul Fowler. I had the same tests,' Paul butted in quickly.

'Ah yes. It seems you both were poisoned with arsenic trioxide.'

'What?' Eve exclaimed. 'Is that any different to ordinary arsenic?'

'Oh yes,' the doctor replied. 'It's used to treat different cancers, in particular leukaemia. However, whoever gave it to you gave you a big overdose. I don't think it was intended to kill you, but to make you very sick.'

'It certainly did that,' Paul commented.

'Have you any idea how he or she got it?' the doctor asked. 'It's a prescription drug.'

'The person who gave it to us — ' Paul explained, ' — his mum had leukaemia. He must have had some left over.'

Eve noticed that Dimitris Kastrinakis

was standing at the door. She wondered how long he'd been there. The doctor turned and looked at Dimitris. 'Could this have killed them?' Dimitris asked.

'It's not likely, though the other lady is very ill. If they had been left for a long time, their chances would not have been so good.'

Eve shivered, but she knew David would have come to save her.

'Well, Miss Masters, I hope that this will be the last time you get involved in a murder,' Dimitris spoke.

I knew it — I knew he couldn't keep himself from saying something, she thought. However, she decided not to give him the pleasure of seeing her react. 'Any luck in finding James yet?' she asked instead.

'I'm afraid not,' he replied. 'But we will. Believe me, we will.'

Eve wasn't so sure, however.

* * *

Paul went and sat at Jane's bedside. She was asleep and looked peaceful, but he knew that when she woke, all the awful memories would come flooding back. He wanted to make them go away, but he didn't know if he would be able to or if she would let him.

Ten minutes later, Jane's eyes slowly opened. She saw Paul sitting there and she smiled.

'You're all right, then?' she asked.

'I'm not too bad. I'll only have to be in hospital for a couple of days.'

'And Eve?'

'The same.'

'Thank goodness,' she said, breathing a sigh of relief.

'Don't worry about us,' Paul said, taking her hand. 'It's you we're all anxious about. Your reaction to the injection was the worst out of all of us.' He was delighted when Jane didn't take her hand away.

'I'm sure I'll be fine,' she said, but then suddenly burst into tears.

Paul didn't know what to do. 'Jane, oh, I'm so sorry. I know this is horrible for you. I wish I could help you.'

'You have, Paul,' she said, the tears subsiding. 'You really have. I felt so much better with you in that room. I felt I could cope.'

'But it was such a shock for you. How could you ever trust another man?'

Jane smiled. 'Paul, of course it was a shock, and I couldn't believe it. I don't know if I'll ever get over what James did, but I don't believe all men are like that.'

'Good.'

Jane looked tired and drawn and Paul wondered if he should leave. 'You look like you should get some more rest,' he said.

'I am tired, but can you sit with me for a while, unless you need to rest yourself.'

'I'm feeling a lot better and I'd love to sit with you for a while.'

Jane closed her eyes again, hoping not to dream about James. He had hurt her more than she wanted to admit, but she refused to think about him any more. She had the opportunity to be with someone who truly cared for her now and she was going to take this chance. However, she would move slowly this time and not rush into the relationship without thinking.

* * *

In an Athens hotel room James came out of the shower, a towel wrapped around his waist. 'So what do you think we should do now?' he asked the woman on the bed. She was around thirty, blonde and quite slim.

'I'm thinking about it,' she said crossly. 'You know that you completely blew it. Not only would we have had Jennifer's money, but eventually Jane's. We've got to get out of Greece, but that won't be easy. The police will be looking for you.'

'I'm sure you'll think of something, darling. You always do,' James said, pushing the woman down on the bed and kissing her passionately.

17

Two days later, David and Eve went for a drink in the Black Cat with Paul and his brother Kevin. Lucy also went with them, having decided to put the past behind her. Eve had been through an awful lot after all.

Both Eve and Paul had been released from hospital that morning and were still feeling a little fragile, but they were glad to be home. Unfortunately, Jane was still confined to the hospital and would be there for at least another week. She and Paul had been getting on well and he hoped James was fading from her memory.

When they entered the bar, Annie saw them straight away and called them over. Betty and Don were sitting at the same table and Eve realised she hadn't seen Betty for ages. Surprisingly, she almost missed their unfriendly banter.

'Wonderful to see you two up and about,' Annie said to Eve and Paul.

'Any news about James?' Don asked.

'I'm afraid not,' Eve replied.

'Must be frightening, wondering if he's going to come back to finish the job,' Betty put in.

Here she goes again, thought Eve. *The harbinger of doom*.

'Oh, I doubt he'll be back,' David put in quickly, not wanting an argument to start. 'If he'd have wanted to kill them, he would have done it in the first place.'

Betty grunted. She was rapidly going off David. He supported Eve way too often.

'That's right,' Paul added. 'He realised he couldn't kill us all and get rid of the bodies, so he poisoned us to give him time to escape.'

'I only hope they find him,' Eve said. 'It'll give us peace of mind. Not that I think he'll try anything here again, but he may attempt to fool some other poor souls.'

'Not like you to be concerned for

other people, Eve,' Betty commented.

Eve found her temper rising, but she wasn't going to give that woman the satisfaction, she wasn't . . .

'Now what are we having to drink?' Paul asked, hoping to defuse the situation.

Eve was relieved that he'd butted in, as she had nearly responded to Betty's nasty comment. She wanted to have a nice peaceful day and keep David in a good mood. He deserved it after all the angst she'd put him through. She asked for a gin and tonic and went and sat down next to Annie, completely ignoring Betty.

David was impressed by Eve's behaviour and was getting fed up with Betty. He decided to keep away from her and went to sit down between Don and Pete. Lucy sat next to Betty, but even she felt the woman was being unfair to Eve.

As they were drinking and chatting, Dimitris came in and immediately walked over to them.

'Ah, I thought I'd find you here, Miss

Masters. I have some news.'

What on earth does he mean by that? Does he think I'm an alcoholic? she thought angrily. However, although Eve was insulted by this remark, she was also excited that he had news. 'What, about James?' she asked.

'Yes, James Anderson has been found dead in a hotel room in Athens. He died of strychnine poisoning.'

They all gasped and Eve was the first to speak. 'Have they caught who did it?'

'No, and I don't know if they will. The room was booked to a woman, a Diane Harris, but she had a forged passport which she left at the check-in desk. Of course this might not even be her real name. The body of James Anderson was found by the cleaning people this morning, but the time of death was yesterday evening. She is long gone.'

'Well, she's done us all a favour,' Eve said.

'But she's still committed a crime,' Dimitris commented.

Eve shrugged her shoulders. James

was an evil man in her opinion and deserved no sympathy.

'I must go and tell Jane,' Paul said. 'I don't know how she will react.'

'One of my officers has gone to the hospital,' Dimitris told him.

'Oh no, I'll need to be with her.' Paul rushed out, leaving his drink hardly touched.

'I don't understand,' Dimitris said. 'After what that man did to her.'

'She was in love with him,' Eve said haughtily.

Dimitris shook his head and left the bar. He would never understand the English.

'So, Eve, another murder over,' Pete said. 'What are you going to do to pass the time now?'

'I'm going to start an amateur theatre group. Who's in?' she asked, surprising everyone, particularly David, who was delighted she'd found something safe to do with her time.

Annie and Don immediately said they wanted to join and then Lucy said she'd like to do backstage work. Betty glared at Eve.

That woman. Always trying to take centre stage. It'll never work. Never.

* * *

Paul paused before entering Jane's ward. Her ward also had only four people in it and he could see Jane in the far corner. Finally he got up the courage and went in, slowly approaching her bed. 'Hello, Jane,' he whispered. He could see she'd been crying. Perhaps there wasn't any hope for them after all.

'Paul! I didn't expect to see you here tonight.'

'The police inspector came into the bar this evening with the news about James.'

'Oh.'

'How are you?'

'I'm okay, I think. It came as a bit of a shock.' A few tears started to fall and she got out a hanky. Paul stood there nervously, not knowing what to do. Jane could sense his awkwardness. 'I'm not crying because I still love him, Paul. I'm crying because . . . oh, I don't know. It's all been so horrible and sad and such a mess. I feel confused. I'm sorry.'

'I'm sorry too,' Paul said. 'Here I am pushing myself onto you when you need time.'

'Paul, you've been lovely; you haven't been pushy at all. I do need to take things slowly, but please stay.'

Paul happily sat down and took Jane's hand. She looked so young and vulnerable. How could that man have treated her like he had? He wanted to put his arms around her and hold her to him, but it was too soon.

'I wonder who that woman was?' she asked.

'I have no idea.'

'It sounds like she was the mastermind behind the whole plan.'

'It does,' Paul agreed. 'And when he came back with nothing, she got rid of him. It almost makes me feel sorry for him.'

'No, Paul. He doesn't deserve any pity. He knew what he was doing. If everything had gone to plan, I would have been his next victim. He would have married me and after a decent amount of time, poisoned me so he could inherit my money. He would probably have used arsenic in small doses so I'd gradually get sicker and sicker and finally die. On top of everything, I expect James was in a relationship with that woman.'

'Jane, you've got to stop thinking like this and about what could have happened. It's all over.'

'I know. I'll be fine. I promise.'

Paul wasn't sure. He had to find some way to cheer her up and give her hope. 'When you get out of here, perhaps we can go out for dinner?' he asked nervously, hoping this wasn't moving too fast.

'I'd love that,' she replied.

Paul was delighted. He'd do everything he could to make her forget that terrible man. Then, all of a sudden, Jane reached over and kissed him, surprising him completely.

Perhaps it wouldn't be as difficult as he imagined. Now all he had to do was persuade Jane to come and live in Crete!

* * *

Betty peered in through the window of the Black Cat. It was ten o'clock on a Monday morning in early February. *Everybody's there. I don't believe it. It's going to be a shambles, mark my words. That I can say for certain.*

Eve had kept her promise and had started an amateur theatre group. Ken and Jan had offered their bar in the mornings for rehearsals and she'd managed to get the local school for the actual performances. She'd had a great response when she'd advertised for people to join, both as actors and for work behind the scenes. Ken, Jan, Annie, Pete, Don, Lucy, Kevin, Paul and Jane all joined immediately.

Lucy and Kevin found they were

getting on a little better with this new interest in their lives, and Paul and Jane's relationship was going from strength to strength. She hadn't committed to staying in Crete for the rest of her life, but she had given up her job in England and hadn't bought an air ticket back to the UK yet.

Betty was fuming when Don joined the group, despite knowing how much he loved the theatre. However, he didn't care, having become a more confident man who was now much less under his wife's thumb.

A few Greeks who spoke English well also joined, including Petros, John Phillips's old foreman. Dimitris thought about it, but decided he couldn't cope with Eve on a regular basis.

David, who had been a professional actor, also offered his services. He normally wouldn't be interested in amateur dramatics, but he felt he had to support Eve. He was proud of her decision to start this group.

'It's such a relief you've got a new

interest, darling, even if you are putting on a murder mystery! I knew you couldn't avoid the subject completely.'

'It is rather exciting putting on my own production, David.'

However, Eve wasn't enjoying it quite as much as she thought she would. David was the only professional actor there and he was excellent, but most of the others weren't. It was tiring and frustrating. Eve was starting to get bored again and was longing for another crime to solve. It didn't have to be murder; any major crime would do. All memories of being tied up and poisoned had disappeared, and being a private detective sounded thrilling again.

As Annie stumbled over her lines and Lucy put out the wrong props, Eve drifted into her dream world again. A professional make-up artist was working on her eyes and she was pleased with how she looked. She was excited and the enthusiasm showed in her face. In no more than half an hour she would be interviewed by the BBC, having solved yet another horrendous crime. She couldn't wait to go through all the details with the reporter and then wait for the congratulations.

Eve closed her eyes, imagining that moment, but then there was an almighty crash. She jumped up and saw Pete on the floor. He had fallen over a chair which had been full of props. He managed to get up and when everyone saw he was all right, they started laughing. Eve shook her head. *What have I go myself into*? she thought.

Eve looked at David and realised she was doing this for him. She loved him and didn't want to lose him . . . but solving real crimes was so much more exciting than play acting, wasn't it?

Now, wouldn't it be fun to find out who killed James Anderson?

THE END